Heaven Between Her Thighs:

Stealing His Heart

By

Denora M. Boone

Remember….

You haven't read 'til you've read #Royalty

Acknowledgements

Never will I ever fail to tell God thank you! If it wasn't for Him choosing me to be on this journey, I don't know where I would be. With each book He gives me, He continues to show me my growth in not just writing, but spiritually as well. I still have a lot of growing to do but I know that with Him guiding me I won't fail.

My husband and my best friend, Byron. I know you love me because this writer's life is no joke, and it takes a strong man to love an author! We are moody when we get writer's block, we think our characters are real, and we work serious trap hours. You know all times of night and stuff! Lol!! But you support me and that's big for me. Thank you, baby, for sacrificing to make sure that I'm walking in my calling.

Jalen, Elijah, Mekiyah, and Isaiah, Mommy does this for you! I want to make sure that everything I do now will cause each of you to be more successful than me and Daddy. I pray that God blesses each of you abundantly and that we are here every step of the way.

Charles and Jenica Johnson, what can I say? The two of you are awesome! God used y'all in a tremendous way and I don't know how many times I can thank you for all that you have done. Not just business wise, but in our personal lives. Blood really couldn't make us any closer and I love you!

My AIP family!!!! Boy we may be small but we are powerful, and I thank God for each and every one of you. Every decision I make is to benefit us all. I don't want to leave anyone behind, and as we grow and God sends us more family members, just know that my love will never change. Thank you for believing in me!

Pastor Carlos and Chenille White and my Kingdome Dominion Ministries family, I adore you all. I feel like my family and I have been there forever instead of only a few months, and that's all because of how you welcomed us and loved us. We are so grateful and I pray that everything that your hearts desire, God blesses you with it.

Porscha Sterling and my new Royalty family, thank you for having me. I am blessed to be a part of such a wonderful group of women who wants to see everyone succeed. Regardless of my past, you saw beyond that and opened the door for me. I pray that I can continue to make you proud.

Latisha Smith Burns, sis, you did that! I love and appreciate you just for who you are in my life. You make sure that everyone connected to you is good and in return, I will always do the same for you. Now if we can get you to stop fussing so much then we would be good! Ha!

I know I'm going to forget someone but I promise it's not intentional. But to Deedy Smith, Krystal Sheppard, Deja McCullough, Fanita Moon Pendleton (the best big sis ever), Patrice A'zayler Watts, Yoshi Chance (the best cousin ever), Tanechea Renea Merida, Jade Crystal, and Lorrell 'Plez Her' Wilkerson (the best big brother ever) I thank you all for riding with me like you do. I love y'all so much and each of you have a place in my heart!

To my readers!!! You are the real MVPs, and as long as God gives me I will give you all. I love you!!

Now let's get into this here tea!

"Daughters of Jerusalem, do not arouse or awaken love until it so desires." Song of Song 8:4

1

"REE!" Trinity yelled from her bedroom door.

Looking over at the bed where her on again off again boyfriend slept peacefully, she couldn't stop the rage she felt on the inside. Trinity knew that she deserved better than what he was giving her but for the last three years, she had been settling because she really did love him. Today, unlike the many days before, she felt like they had finally come to their end, if he didn't have a logical explanation for what she had just stumbled upon.

"QYREE! Get up 'cause I know you hear me," she yelled again. This time she moved closer so that she could get right over his head. There was no way that he was going to continue to sleep like he didn't have a care in the world, while her heart felt like it was being ripped out of her chest.

"Man, Trin, go head on with all that yelling," he mumbled.

All he needed was a few more minutes of sleep before he headed out to make his rounds for the day. The last thing he needed was for Trinity to interrupt that process and cause him to have a bad attitude for the rest of the day.

"Nah punk, you got some explaining to do. Who is Natalia? And don't tell me she's your cousin like Carmen, Kalina, and Teria!"

This bit of information got his attention. For Trinity to call out his new side piece's name only meant one thing. She had gone through his phone yet again. Time after time he had told her to stop invading his privacy because he was a grown man, but for the life of her she couldn't just play her position.

Instead of responding to her, he uncovered his head and looked her over. He had to admit that Trinity was a bad one. Her light skin complexion, big pretty hazel eyes, and stacked body was what caught his attention when he first met her back in the day. She kept a fresh hairdo and her clothes were always up to par. Right now, she was rocking her hair in a short cut with curls on the top and the ends dyed a deep purple. Lil mama was definitely a keeper; Qyree just didn't want to be the one to keep her.

Qyree Reeves didn't have a faithful bone in his body. When it came to women, he only saw them good for one thing and that was what they held between their legs. Other than that, they could kick rocks. Yeah, he may have filled up their heads with hopes and dreams of one day him being a one-woman man, but had they been able to recognize game, then they would have saved themselves the heartache that he was sure to give them. His 'hit it and quit it' game was strong!

Slightly pushing Trinity out of the way so that he could make it to the bathroom, he heard her suck her teeth from behind him. Whatever she had seen or heard about his new flavor of the month had her deep in her feelings and he just wasn't in the mood.

Finishing up his business, he reached over to get his wash rag and toothbrush so that he could handle his morning ritual. Qyree looked at himself in the mirror and couldn't help but to smile at the person that stared back at him. He knew why the women flocked to him, how could they not? Standing at an even six feet, his thick built frame was covered in caramel colored skin and was full of tattoos. His hair was cut low with waves spinning, and a long thick beard that he was known for. The ladies loved it so he used it to his advantage.

Qyree made his way back out to the bedroom that was attached to the master bath, and saw that Trinity had left his phone on the bed. Glancing over at his screen he smirked, noticing she left it on the message thread between he and Natalia, and shook his head. Women just couldn't seem to mind their own business when it came to men's personal items but then wanted to get an attitude when they found what they were looking for. He just didn't understand them but nevertheless, he was still unbothered. If Trinity wanted to remove herself from the roster than she could most definitely do so. He would just get another one to play her position.

Instead of taking his shower there, Qyree decided to just get dressed and head to his house before hitting the streets. Redressing in his red Polo shirt, dark blue True Religion jeans, and his red and blue retro Jordans he grabbed his phone and keys to head out.

Trinity was sitting in the living room going off on her phone about him like it would move him. He already knew who she was talking to and what was being said on the other end about him. Tonya lived for the gossip that Trinity brought to her about him, but what Trinity failed to realize was that Tonya used that to her advantage.

Everything that Trinity ran back and told, Tonya made sure to stash that bit of knowledge in her mind so that she wouldn't do the same things Qyree hated. That's right; Tonya was on the roster, too, and Trinity was clueless.

Shaking his head. he didn't even bother to let her know he was leaving, he just swaggered his way to his Benz and hopped in. By the time Qyree had the car in reverse, Trinity must have realized he was no longer in the house because she stepped out on the porch yelling and carrying on. She knew he hated when she made a scene in public especially since she lived in the hood. It was always some birds lurking around waiting on something to pop off.

Turning up the demo of an up and coming artist in the area, he headed down the street towards the stop sign. He didn't know what made him look in his rearview mirror but when he did, he couldn't help the laughter that erupted from his body. Trinity was running full speed ahead down the sidewalk, yelling and cursing him out he imagined. It was definitely time for her to go on punishment yet again, and after a few days he knew she would get her act together. The only reason he even entertained her was because of what she offered and it wasn't her mind. Out of all of his women her heaven, as he called it, was the best he had ever had. But that still wasn't good enough for him to be with only her. Unlike his father, he was never getting married and if none of his women understood that, they could kick rocks.

Looking into his rearview one last time he shook his head and hit the gas. It was time to get to the money and playing around with Trinity wasn't adding to his pockets.

2

Sitting in her office, Cheynese Broadus took a sip from her coffee mug as she went over the file of the parolee that she had just been assigned to. Cheynese loved her job as a parole officer, regardless of how difficult some of the people were that she interacted with on the daily. Some received her and some didn't, but instead of her casting out judgement, she tried to see things from their points of view in order to try and help them. If they didn't learn anything from her, she was sure to learn something from them.

She had just moved back home to Valdosta to be closer to her family. California was nice and all, but it just didn't give her that homey feeling she was longing for. It was a blessing that she could just transfer her job since there was an opening and she wouldn't have to be out of work long, searching. God was always on time and she was grateful for that.

Turning the page in the file, she came across the mugshot of the woman. Vonetta Simms had been locked up the last five years for being a co-conspirator and accessory to the rape of her then best friend, Nivea Davis. She was only 17 at the time of her conviction and she would have been out on her twenty-first birthday, had she not gotten into so much trouble the first two years she was locked up. It seemed like she racked up more charges behind bars then when she was out on the street. Now at 27, she had finally learned her lesson and was tired of living the life that she had been for so long.

Reading over the file, Cheynese started to understand the reasons behind why Vonetta carried on the way she had. The life she was accustomed to wasn't one that she would have wished on her worst enemy. The things that girl faced at the hand of the people that were supposed to protect her, caused her to lash out the way she did. Not giving Von an excuse for what she had done, but Cheynese was now able to understand where she went wrong.

"Ms. Broadus, your next appointment is here," her assistant spoke over the intercom.

"Thanks, you can bring her on back."

Not even a full minute later, Rosalin opened the door and ushered Von inside. The woman looking back at her was not the same girl she had just seen in that mugshot. Instead of an angry, mean, and hurt child, there stood a strong, healed, and beautiful young lady. Chey could tell that this change was only one that could be done by God Himself, and she silently thanked Him for doing a new thing in this woman.

Von had put on a significant amount of weight from what she could tell, but it wasn't in a bad way. Her hair was natural and sat on top of her head in a cute twist out style. Her cocoa colored skin was blemish free and her dark brown eyes and button nose brought out her other facial features. Dressed down in some dark blue jeans, a red sweater, and some black flats, she didn't look a day over sixteen.

"Good morning. I'm Cheynese Broadus," Chey said as she walked over to shake Von's hand.

"Cheynese? Like the food and language?"

Chey couldn't help but to laugh because there wasn't a day that went by where she got the same reaction from people when she told them her name. When she was younger, she hated her name and even went home crying on quite a few occasions, because the kids were picking on her name. But now that she was older, she embraced it because it was just who she was.

Her mother, Brenda had named her that for two reasons. One, was because she loved Chinese food and when Chey was born, her eyes were so slanted that she looked Asian. Her long thick hair that stopped in the middle of her back, along with her light skin often made people think she was mixed, but both of her parents were African American. As genetics would have it, she took after her late grandmother in the looks department instead of either of her parents.

"Yes. Just like both," Chey laughed.

Once Rosalin left the two alone, Chey decided to get right to everything. She only had a few things to discuss, to make sure that Von was ready to go to the halfway house and understood all of the terms of her release.

"So… you ready to make this transition?" Chey asked her.

"More than ever. I'm so excited to be able to see my son, Amir," Von beamed.

Chey had read that Von had a young son and had been praying that Von was one of the mothers that got out and really took her freedom seriously this time. She had run into so many cases where the mothers were ready to get back to their kids and declared that they would never return back to what caused them to be taken away in the first place, only to go back months later. It always broke Chey's heart when that happened, so she tried her best to be as much support as she could, especially to the women that didn't have any. Good support was one of the most important things that a person could have returning back to society, and the ones who didn't always ended back up at square one.

"I'm glad to hear that. If there is one thing I would suggest would be to think of him every time you get tempted to do something that you know isn't right. You wouldn't believe the women and men that come through my office ready to get back to their families, only to leave them again. And not all are lost to jail either," Chey told her, praying that she got her drift.

"I understand what you're saying. There have been a few women that I was locked up with who got out and came right back. Every time that would happen, I prayed harder that God wouldn't let that be my fate. I already have something else that may take me away from Amir before he's an adult."

Hearing that she was a praying woman made Chey happy, but as soon as she saw the tears forming in Von's eyes when she told her something else could take her away from her baby, it made her feel bad as well.

"What could possibly take you away from him besides you getting caught back up in the system again?"

"I'm HIV positive," she said.

Chey was pretty sure that information was in her records but by her just getting the file not too long ago, she hadn't had the chance to go through it all. It was scary how true it was that you couldn't tell if a person was sick just by looking at them. Just from Von's appearance, you couldn't tell she was sick, but none of that mattered to Chey. To her, Von was another human being who deserved another chance at life, and she was going to do all that she could for her in order to help her succeed.

"Well, we will pray and I will touch and agree that you will be here long enough to see even your grandbabies," Chey smiled as Von thanked her for that.

"So what all do I need to do in order to be able to see him while I'm at the halfway house?" Von wanted to know. The both of them were getting misty eyed and the last thing she wanted to do was waste time by crying. She had spent too many days and nights crying, so now it was time to celebrate.

After another 45 minutes of getting Von everything she needed for her transition to go smoothly, she was ready to go.

"So do you have any more questions for me?"

"Just one," Von said looking a little nervous.

"Sure, go ahead."

"Would you mind being with me when I get to see my son for the first time?"

Chey was shocked that she wanted her there for such an intimate family moment, but after getting to know Von a little more, she understood. It was going to be tough to see her son after all of these years, and the fact that the same woman she went to jail behind was the same one who was raising her son, had to be tough.

When Von told Chey that Nivea and her husband, Terrance were raising her son, along with their other two children, to say she was shocked was an understatement. It could only be God that had their hearts open to receive that precious little boy whose mother was behind bars for violating in the worst way. Chey definitely needed to be there to not only be that support she needed, but to see exactly who these people were. Things like that were just unheard of.

"I wouldn't mind at all. Just call me with the details and I will make sure that I am there," Chey told her.

Once Von left, Chey skimmed over the rest of her file to make sure that nothing was left out. She only had one more appointment for the day, but that wasn't scheduled until after lunch. That was right on time because the way her stomach was set up, she was being disrespectful by not feeding it, and she knew just what to get to please it.

"Rosalin, can you order me some lunch, please?"

"Shrimp fried rice, sesame chicken, two egg rolls, and a sprite?"

"You got it," Chey laughed. Thanks to her mother, she had it bad for all things related to China and their cuisine.

3

Qyree walked into his parents' massive home and headed straight for his side of the house. At 26 years old, you would think that he would have been out of his parents' home, but he didn't see a reason to. His parents spoiled him since he was the only child and the life he lived afforded him the luxuries he had become accustomed to. He didn't have to spend his own money unless he wanted to, and he wasn't about to pay to live in someone else's home, if he could be there or at one of his jump-offs for free. The only time he would move out and purchase his own home was when he got married, and he vowed to the death of him that wasn't happening. Why buy the cow when you can get the milk for free?

"What's good, old man?" Qyree greeted his father when he walked past his office and saw him sitting behind his big oak desk.

His father, Jaxon Reeves, was the CEO to one of the largest record labels in the music industry. He had started his company from the ground up almost 30 years ago and he had gone nowhere but up. Everybody wanted to be signed to Hype Lyfe Records, but not just anybody would be. Jaxon made sure only to sign the hottest up and coming artists and when it came to making hits, he was that deal.

"What's good my boy?" Jaxon may have been going on 55, but he didn't look a day over 35.

The few gray hairs he had didn't take away from his boyish look; it only enhanced his look. That six-five frame of his with the bulging muscles, dark skin, light brown eyes, and dimple in his chin made him stand out in any crowd. When Jaxon Reeves walked in a room, his presence commanded attention and he was sure to get it. Especially from the ladies. Qyree had learned from the best when it came to the women. Jaxon had taught him all that he knew and was proud of the masterpiece he had created.

"Chillin'. 'Bout to shower and head over to the office to check on things before falling through this new chick's spot."

"Oh word? You put a new one on the roster?" Jaxon laughed.

"You already know how I do," Qyree bragged.

"Indeed. Let me know what her mama looks like and maybe we can go on a double date." Jaxon fell out laughing. They may have been laughing about it, but Qyree knew just how serious his father was. It was nothing for the two of them to hook up with a mother and daughter then move on to the next.

After chopping it up for a few more minutes and getting some info from his father that he needed to take to the office, Qyree headed towards his initial destination. Just like before, he stopped to talk, only this time it was to his mother. She was alone in her bedroom, kneeling down at the foot of her bed with her head down. Once he heard her say 'Amen', he knew that she was praying.

"What's going on, gorgeous?"

"Hey handsome," she smiled.

Qyree's mother, Zaria was a beautiful woman inside and out. She was a short little something with her flawless dark skin, short hair that she kept naturally curly; her lips were full and her eyes were the prettiest shade of brown Qyree had ever seen in his life. But her eyes showed nothing but sadness any time she looked at him and he knew exactly why.

"What you doing in the house instead of out shopping or hanging with Auntie Zina?"

Walking over to him, she embraced him before maneuvering her way back to the bench that sat at the foot of her bed.

"I just needed some time to talk to the Lord, baby," she said looking out of the window.

"Everything alright?" Qyree asked having an idea of what was wrong.

Looking up at him, Zaria gave a weak smile. If there was one woman in this world that he would give his all to, it was his mother. Whenever he saw her like this, he wanted to do whatever he could to make it better, but he knew this wasn't a problem he could fix.

"I'm just tired baby, that's all. Almost 30 years and nothing has changed," she said.

Taking a seat beside her, he placed his arm around her shoulders and pulled her close to him. He loved his father and was just like him, but this was his mother. The first and only woman that he had ever loved and would give his life for. He could never understand why his father felt the need to constantly have affair after affair. It wasn't like she was just a jump-off like the women he ran through but the one who had carried his children and the one he made a vow to God with.

"Why do you stay then, Ma?" he wanted to know.

For years he wondered why his mother stayed with his father when he was blatantly disrespecting her with other women. Qyree remembered like it was yesterday, the first time his father had gotten caught with his pants down. Literally.

***

Twenty Years Ago

Zaria had just left in the car that was supposed to take her to the airport. She had a scheduled flight out to Los Angeles to attend an event with Jaxon. It was last minute because her boss had been tripping about letting her off in time, and she was unsure if she was going to be able to make it.

That was one of the things that Qyree's parents were constantly arguing about. Jaxon wanted her to stay home and let him spoil her, while Zaria loved her job as a Registered Nurse. She felt like that was her calling to be able to help people and she loved every minute of it. Zaria had gotten so many accolades for her excellent and dedicated service as a nurse and she knew that was all God's doing.

Qyree sat in the living room hard at work playing 'Super Smash Bros' on his brand new Nintendo 64. He was so hype because he had been the first one out of his friends to get it even before it hit stores. His mother had been gone for almost an hour and he was just getting into his game good when he heard the front door open and close. A few seconds later he saw his father come in carrying one of his overnight bags and his driver was bringing in the rest.

"Hey son. What you doing?" Jaxon asked as he walked over to his son.

"Super Smash Bros and it's so cool!"

"I'm glad you like it. Where's Toni?" he asked referring to their live-in nanny. She had been hired not too long ago against Zaria's wishes. So far things were good having her there. She made sure that any and everything that was needed to be done got done in a timely manner, and she loved Qyree like he was her own.

"She's in her room," Qyree said, never taking his eyes off of the television.

Jaxon got up and unbeknownst to Qyree headed straight for her room and shut the door behind him. Qyree paused the game because he heard what sounded like bumping into a wall. Making his way to the hall he did his best to pinpoint where it was coming from.

He and his parents' bedrooms were upstairs, and there was a spare bed downstairs right off of the living room. The knocking wasn't faint but it was still loud *enough to know that it wasn't coming from the upstairs. Just as he got to Toni's door, he heard his father grunt at the same time the front door was opening again.*

Running down the hallway, he ran right into his mother. Looking up into her face, he saw that she had been crying and a feeling that something wasn't right came over him. It was at that moment that he knew there was about to be a problem.

"Baby, is Daddy home?" Zaria asked kneeling in front of him.

Nodding his head, he told her yes and waited. Zaria was taking slow deep breaths and wiping tear after tear for a few minutes, before she hugged him tight and held on as if her life depended on it.

"Qy, I need you to go to your room and close your door, okay? Don't come out until I tell you to," she instructed.

Without another word, Qyree went in his room like he was asked to do, only to open it slightly after a few seconds. At the angle his room sat at the top of the stairs he could look right down and see Toni's room. He watched as his mother stood there crying silently, as her shoulders shook and she repeatedly opened and closed her hands into tight fists.

Before Qyree could even blink again, his mother had burst into the room and Toni screamed. He couldn't make out what was being said but what he did know was that his father was quiet. He knew Jaxon was in there because he heard him, so why wasn't he talking and trying to calm his mother down?

"This is what we do now, Jaxon? You sleeping with the help!" Zaria yelled as she went after Toni again.

"Get her off of me Jaxon!" Toni screamed as he just stood there with a satisfied smirk on his face.

"You better fight back is all I can tell you."

It wasn't until Qyree burst into the room that Jaxon took control of the situation.

"Get off my mommy!" Qyree said as he tried his best to pull his mother off of his babysitter. Why was Miss Toni naked, he wondered, and why was his father putting his clothes back on in a hurry?

Pulling the two of them apart, Qyree could now see that he probably should have been helping Miss Toni because her face was all bruised and scratched up and his mother didn't have a hair out of place. He watched as Toni scrambled to get her body covered, while his mother walked over and slapped the life out of his father.

"Again, Jax?"

Looking at Zaria, Jaxon walked over to where Toni was now sitting fully dressed.

"You did this?" he asked her.

"I sure did. I'm tired of playing these games with you and waiting on you to leave her so we can be together," Toni boldly stated.

"Baby girl, let me tell you something. I will never be replaced and especially not by you. If it wasn't for us hiring you, you wouldn't have a pot to piss in or a window to throw it out of," Zaria spoke up.

"Oh really? Tell her, Jaxon. Tell her how you are tired of her putting her job and church before her family. Tell her how you told me that now since I'm pregnant you have a reason to leave for good this time.

"Pregnant?" Zaria whispered.

It was at that moment that Qyree saw his father's ears produce smoke because he was so mad. He didn't understand what all of this meant but he knew what pregnant was. His father was indeed having a baby by someone that wasn't his mother.

SLAP!

The force of the slap that landed across Jaxon's face from Zaria's hand had probably rearranged the nerves in his whole head. That's just how much power it had behind it.

"Not only have you broken our vows but you got your mistress pregnant too?"

There was no sadness in her voice or face for that matter like it was a few minutes ago. It was now unadulterated anger and it had taken over.

"You have two minutes to get your stuff and get out of my house," Zaria told Toni but kept her eyes fixed on her husband.

"I'm not going anywhere unless Jaxon tells me to," Toni said defiantly.

Turning around slowly like the girl in the movie 'The Exorcist', Zaria gave Toni the look of death before she spoke in a voice that Qyree had never in his life heard before. His mother was always so sweet and loving and now she was in here fussing and fighting. And it was all at the hands of his father.

"You can walk out or you can get bodied and carried out. The choice is yours."

Before Toni could respond Jaxon stepped in.

"You heard my wife. Better hurry up too because you're down to a minute and ten seconds," he said folding his arms and leaning up against the dresser.

"Really Jaxon? You gonna treat me like this? After all of the nights you lay beside me and confess your love for me and our unborn child. Filling my head with the hopes of us being a real family. Telling me how she puts God and her job before you," Toni revealed.

"Oh, so this is what you told her Jaxon? When will you come up with something different to tell your harem?"

The look on Toni's face was complete shock at the revelation of not being Jaxon's only woman. But Jaxon was even more shocked than she was, to know that Zaria knew about the others.

Laughing, Zaria continued. "Yes, Jaxon darling, I know about Megan and Kimberly. They made sure I knew too by constantly calling or coming to my job. I guess they thought by doing that I would leave you and let them step in and take my place. Let's be clear," Zaria said looking over at Toni, "I'm the one with the last name, the house, the child, and the bank accounts. Jaxon will never leave me because it was me that helped him start this record company with the money from the job and prayer from the God that I love so much. You are nothing but something to do and he will never respect you."

"You mean like he respects you by sleeping with other women? You're no better than I am because you share him with me. Obviously, everything that you

mentioned having still doesn't make him want to be faithful," Toni retorted.

As true as that statement was, Zaria wasn't about to give her the satisfaction of knowing it.

"Your time's up and you need to leave," was all she said. There was nothing left to say because in that moment it didn't matter. Once again, Jaxon had broken yet another promise that he would never do this again, but he had.

Grabbing Qyree's hand, Zaria walked to the stairs and began to head in the direction of his room, as he looked over his shoulder at Toni screaming and kicking to avoid being thrown out on her behind.

"I'm sorry you had to see that, baby. Just know that everything will work out and God will fix this, okay?" Zaria explained once they were in his room.

Once again nodding his little head, Qyree was confused. How could the God they sat up in church on

Sundays and Wednesdays and whenever else they wanted to call a meeting, be the same one to allow this to happen to his family?

Before his mother could say anything else, his father was walking in and grabbed her arm, pulling her up. He motioned for her to go into the room they shared with one another and she obliged. Qyree looked up at his father as he smiled and winked at him, like the last fifteen minutes had never happened. It was at that moment that he realized this would be his norm.

***

He would never forget that night as he listened to his parents argue and fight about other women and he had a hard time going to sleep. It felt like he had just drifted off when his mother came in his room waking him up for school the next day. The smile she held on her face no longer reached her eyes, and those were the same sad eyes he looked into at that very moment.

"The reasons I stay, you may not ever understand, Qy," Zaria answered his question, bringing him back to the moment.

He loved his mother and knew his father did too, but Qyree sometimes didn't feel sorry for her as much as he used to. His father was a dog and he knew this because Jaxon had taught him everything he knew; including the fact that if a woman let you play her and never left then there was no reason to stop doing what it was that he wanted.

At first that sounded crazy to him, but over the years as the countless women came and went and his mother stayed, he started believing his father was right. If a woman lets you treat her any kind of way and at the end of the day won't leave, she has no one to blame but herself. A man could only do what a woman allowed him to.

Qyree kissed his mother on the cheek and headed back to his original mission of showering so that he could handle his business.

"Don't end up ruining some girl's life, baby, when you find that one," Zaria said before he got out of her room completely.

"You have nothing to worry about," he said walking off, and that was the truth.

His mother didn't have anything to worry about because he would never settle down. That just wasn't something that he wanted, and he had his father to thank for that. Jaxon taught him how easy it was to get what he wanted from women and not have to have any strings attached.

The only reason Jaxon married Zaria was because she was there before he had anything, and she was the one who put him in position to build his dream. It wasn't until he started getting a name for himself that the women started coming from every direction, and he wanted it no other way. Either Zaria kick rocks or deal with it. And from the looks of things, the latter had been her final answer.

4

Qyree loved his mother but he had to push her to the back of his mind at the moment. Valdosta State University was the school that they decided to hold this year's talent search, held top priority for him. He had heard that some of the hottest undiscovered talent that came out of Valdosta, Georgia and attended that school. If Hype Lyfe could sign at least three of the top artists he had been scoping, this would guarantee his position as the head A&R, something that he had been looking forward to for as long as he could remember. His ear for music was exactly why he was the best for this position, and if he could pull this off then he knew his father would make that happen.

Pulling up to the campus after being on the road for a few hours, he couldn't help the excitement he felt looking at all of the unsuspecting females that walked around. All he could think about was the paradise they held and how he knew he would bag a few before it was all said and done. Besides money and his family, the female body was something he yearned for but he couldn't think about that right now. It was time to get the ball rolling with this event. He had to make sure this show was approved first before he could think about how many he would add to his roster.

Almost an hour and a half later, the meeting was complete and Qyree was heading to his car with one of the biggest smiles on his face that he had ever possessed. As soon as the dean agreed that he could move forward with everything, it was hard for him to sit through the rest of the meeting. They made sure to discuss all of the specifics along with the do's and don'ts. Since they were on campus, they had to make sure that no underage drinking would go on along with having the proper security for the night. None of that was an issue for him because prior to the meeting, they had secured the local police department to be their security. With them there, all of the other possible mishaps should be to a minimum.

"Ssssss," Qyree hissed as he spotted two women walking ahead of him. He couldn't see their faces but that didn't matter. Whatever their faces lacked he was sure their bodies made up for it. Shoot, when the lights were out, it was all the same anyway. Now that his business was done for the day, he could focus on getting him a few new play things. If his luck was good, he would have not just one but both.

He admired them for a minute before catching up to them. They were both on the thick side, which was his favorite, and the way their behinds sat up in their clothes was definitely a plus. Looking at them, he thought that maybe one was someone of importance by the cream business suit she had on, while the other could have just been a regular student. Clad in some jeans and Air Max, she even made the simple outfit stand out.

"Excuse me ladies, can I speak with you for a minute?" he asked, jogging up behind them.

Turning around, he was shocked to see someone from his past, and it was a pleasant surprise. Obviously, she was pleased as well by the smile she wore on her face.

"Omg, Qyree, how are you?" she said closing in the space between the two as she embraced him.

"I'm good. Man, it's been a long time, for real," he told her. "What you doing here?"

"Long isn't the word. This is home for me and I just moved back not too long ago. Oh, I'm so rude. Von, this is Qyree Reeves; we attended USC together," she introduced the two.

"Nice to meet you," Von said. She wasn't rude but Qyree could tell that she wasn't in the mood.

"So what are you doing here?" Chey asked.

"I was just getting the final details for this talent event our company is holding here in two weeks. Trying to put a few people on, ya know?"

"That's right. I forgot about your family's record label. How's that going?"

"It's doing real good. Pops is changing the game right now and hopefully, this will elevate us more," he said as they began walking towards the parking lot. Von walked ahead of them so that she wouldn't be in their business. Something about him rubbed her the wrong way but she didn't know what it was. Maybe the way his eyes roamed over her body when Chey was introducing them. Or maybe she was just tired from dealing with everything for one day.

"That's awesome. God is so worthy. How is your mother?" she asked. While in school, Chey ended up meeting his mother during one of the times his parents came to visit. She would never forget Mrs. Reeves because she was just a beautiful spirit.

"My mother is doing good. She's retired now, so of course she's waiting on me to get married and have her a house full of grandbabies. But look, I will catch up with you later; work calls," Qyree told her after looking at the screen on his vibrating phone. Looking down to see Natalia's picture message let him know that he needed to hurry up 'cause she was ready.

"Alright then. It was good seeing you," Chey responded before getting in her car on the driver's side.

Watching Qyree pull off like a bat out of hell, all she could do was imagine that he was on his way to a woman's house. If he was anything like he used to be when they were in college, her assumptions would be dead on.

5

As Cheynese and Von sat in the third row of the small church, neither of them could deny the presence of God that they both felt. He was definitely letting His anointing fall fresh on each member that was in attendance. The word that was going forth was ministering to their souls and she couldn't get enough.

So much had changed since she had been back home, but her childhood church, His Lighted Path Church of God In Christ, was still the same. Looking around the room, she saw familiar faces, along with people she had never seen before, and that was a good thing because it meant that the ministry was growing.

Tuning back in to what was going on with the message, she had just picked up on her pastor asking her to come and give them a selection. It had been years since she sang in a church but this shouldn't have come as a surprise to her, considering her pastor was also her father.

Getting up, she politely excused herself from the pew and walked up to where her father was standing.

"You're not slick," she laughed at him as he winked and kissed her cheek before taking his seat.

"To God be the glory," she said closing her eyes and raising her right hand in worship. "It's been a long time since I have been up here but it feels so good. Being away from home for so long, I had my fair share of struggles, but God was there to see me through it all. So getting up here and lifting my voice unto Him is a praise that I owe to Him. Can I get an Amen somebody?"

"Amen," came from almost everyone in the sanctuary, including Von. It had been so long since she had been able to be in church and for a long time, she was mad at God for something that she had caused. But with time and understanding of what He was trying to do in her life, she surrendered everything to Him and didn't turn back. So the struggles Chey was talking about, she understood because she had her own.

"Won't you all stand to your feet and just begin to give God some praise in this place. Forget about everyone else and just focus on the Master's face as you just love on Him. Let Him know how grateful you are for all that he has done," Chey said before she began her worship to the Lord.

"There's a miracle in this room with my name on it. Glory to God. There's a healing in this room and it's here for me. If you know your healing is here today go ahead and claim it right now. There's a breakthrough in this room and it's got my name on it. So I'm gonna put a praise on it!"

Chey sang the popular Tasha Cobbs song "Put A Praise On It". Von knew that Tasha was a beast when it came to singing but Chey was definitely giving her a run for her money.

The anointing that this woman held and that sickening run that she had just slayed, had every hand up and every eye wet from tears. God definitely had a hand on this woman's life and Von was glad that He had placed her in her life.

By the time she had finished, people were at the altar giving their lives over to Christ and making a vow with our Father to not turn back to their old ways. Of course, some were just going through formality, but there were others that had finally gotten sick and tired of playing with the devil and meant what they had just confessed, Von included. It was at that moment that she decided if God would accept her again, she wasn't turning back. Her son Amir's life depended on it.

Once church was over and everyone was filing out, it seemed like Chey was getting stopped every few feet because someone wanted to welcome her back home, or let her know how beautifully she sang. She was so humble and just kept giving all of the glory to God.

The next day was Von's first day of college and she was a bit nervous, but thanks to Chey and her encouragement when she got dropped off at the halfway house, she was prepared. Getting her high school diploma behind bars was as far as she had gone, but now that she was out and in a different head space, she knew that in order to get where she wanted to be, she had to challenge herself and college would do just that.

Just as Chey made it home and got her things prepared for the week, the release and refilling that she got from attending church a while ago gave her just what she needed to be recharged and ready to go come Monday morning. Standing in her closet, she was having the hardest time picking out something to wear the next day, when her phone rang.

"Hey sissy pooh!" she greeted her best friend.

"Hey honey dip. What you got going on?" Natalia asked her.

"Just got in from church not too long ago and getting things ready for tomorrow," Chey said, still on the hunt for an outfit.

"I knew once you got back you would be at that church house every time the doors open," she cackled.

"Mm hmm, and your behind needs to be right there beside me. Better yet, you need to bring a pillow and blanket and just lay at the altar until you get delivered," Cheynese shot back with a laugh.

"Oh no ma'am. After all those years of my parents dragging me to church, I have had enough. That should be enough to get me inside the pearly gates when it's time to kick the bucket."

"You sound like a whole fool with that logic," Chey said and they both laughed.

"Well, you know what the Bible says somewhere round third Peter, 'Thou God loves all fools and babies' so I'm a shoe in."

"Hunty, whatever Bible you read that in I need you to return it and get your money back. That's not even in one scripture and Peter only has two books. This is why you need to come and get taught and learn the word on your own," she laughed.

"Anywaysss, how does it feel being back home?" Natalia asked.

"It's good. You know I love being home. When you coming to visit since I'm back?"

"I don't know. You know no matter when I pop up, it's always some drama with Mama and Daddy," she said, shrugging her shoulders as if Chey could see her.

The lifestyle that she chose to live over the one her parents tried their best instilling in her was always the topic of discussion, and Natalia wasn't here for it. If she could just go home and be accepted for who she was instead of who she wasn't by their standards, then she would be just fine. Until then, she would continue to do her.

"They only want the best for you and you know that," Chey tried her best to rationalize.

"Yea, well, we'll see. I may come home soon but it's not set in stone and don't quote me on that either. I know how you do."

"I guess I will just have to take a trip to see you when I get some free time then."

"And we gonna turn up when you do, too! Hold on a sec," Natalia told her as she clicked over to her other line.

Cheynese found the perfect outfit with the matching shoes and put them over the back of the bench at the foot of her king size bed, before climbing up to the top. She loved everything about this bed, but she would love it even more when she had someone to share it with. Chey wasn't in a rush to just settle with anyone; she wanted the man that she eventually married to be exactly what God sent to her. All her life she dreamed of the perfect man, but after many failed attempts at relationships, she decided that she would just wait on him to find her.

"I'm back, girl. That was bae and he's on his way over, so I gotta freshen up before he gets here. Call me later this week and let me know if u can make it up this way. Love you, heffa!" Natalia ran off in one breath and ended the call before Chey could say anything back.

Just like always, Natalia was still making men her priority. It may not have been so bad if it was just one, but she had at least one that met each one of her needs. There was one she had to just pay her car note, another for her rent, one for her utilities, and so on. Chey knew she had to be doing them favors as well, but that wasn't for her to call her out on. For as long as they had been friends, Natalia was just fast. People often wondered how they got along so well being they were total opposites, but it was just how they rolled with one another. They were sisters and hopefully one day Chey would rub off on her and she would see her own worth wasn't found in a man.

Settling in with some leftovers and her remote, Chey relaxed and tuned in to some ratchet TV that she had recorded during the week. With her busy schedule, she rarely had time for anything other than church on Thursday nights, so she caught up on her missed episodes on Sunday. She had finished three episodes of *Love and Hip Hop*, but not long after she had gotten through the first half of *How to Get Away with Murder* did her eyes betray her and sleep set in. She would just have to catch up another day.

6

"That's my best friend! You betta, you betta! You want 'em back then come and get ha and ha best friend. Ayeeee." Natalia danced around in front of her bedroom mirror as she got dressed. J. R and Trey Songz knew they had a hit on their hands with that song.

Sticking out her tongue as she twerked around her room, slinging her fresh Peruvian Body Wave sew-in, she knew she was one of the baddest females around. Standing about 5-feet-7, she was a little on the tall side but she loved it. Her body filled out nice in all of the right places, and her Dominican and African American mix gave her that exotic look that drove all of the men crazy. It just wasn't enough to keep the man that she really wanted and she couldn't understand why.

Natalia was a dime; she kept her house clean, she knew how to cook, and she put it down when it came to the intimacy, so for the life of her she couldn't figure out why she couldn't land Qyree like she wanted. Putting some of her Victoria's Secret Bombshell perfume behind her ears and on her wrists, she knew that as soon as he walked into the house and got a whiff of her, it would be on and poppin' like usual. She knew the key to making a man remember you was all about the scent you carried; well, at least that's what her mother taught her. It wasn't all about the price of the perfume but how it complemented your natural body odor. It could cost you $200 a bottle, but if your natural aroma wasn't compatible then you would be walking around still smelling like you just ran a marathon in 100-degree weather.

Looking around the room, Natalia made sure that she had everything in place. The bath water was nice and hot, the candles were lit, she had just put a new comforter set that her sugar daddy Benson had purchased on her bed, and now all she needed was her man. Just as she made sure the silk robe was tied around her body loosely, she heard the front door opening. Knowing that it was only one other person that had access to her house, she eagerly strolled up the hallway.

"Hey baby," she said walking up behind Qyree.

"What's all this for?" he asked turning his nose up.

Paying his attitude no mind, Natalia walked over to him and rubbed her hand up his back. It was something about this man that made her weak whenever she was near him and she couldn't get enough of it. Up until tonight, she had been cool with them just doing what they did when he wanted to without her giving him a hard time, but now she wanted more and it was time she got it.

"Well, when you came over last week you told me you were going to be heading out of town for the weekend, so I wanted to take care of you before you left. I don't need one of those little jailbait broads at that school to try and take what's mine."

"What's yours, huh? You wild, man," was all he said as he headed to the back of the house. He needed to use the bathroom before he got on the road.

Upon entering her bedroom, he saw the little setup she had and groaned inwardly. Not because he was excited, but because he was afraid that this would happen. She had finally caught feelings.

For two years they had been messing around and she was always his favorite jump off. She did her own thing as did he, and she never wanted anything deep between them. That's why when any of his other females were getting too clingy or needy, he would always go to her. He knew right then that he was going to have to pull away before she got any bright ideas about the two of them. Natalia was cool and all but lately, Qyree noticed a change in her all of a sudden, and he couldn't quite put his finger on what it was.

He looked down at his watch as he felt her come up behind him and her skin touch his. Knowing he didn't have much time before he needed to get on the road, he decided he could spare a few more minutes to reach that level of ecstasy he craved. It was like a high that he was constantly chasing. Each woman took him to new heights, but there wasn't one that could be the only one to make him forget about the rest.

Turning around and biting his bottom lip, he knew he was wrong for leaving Trinity in the car, but who cared. Either she sat there until he got done or she could get out and walk home. Either way, he didn't care one bit. She was lucky that he was taking her with him for the show but she had some people down there that could add to his after party and he was all for it. She could get down there and act crazy if she wanted to; she would be hitting the pavement with those big behind feet of hers, trucking it back to Atlanta.

"Hop up, yo," he said to Natalia twenty minutes after being there. He already knew what time it was when he heard his phone ringing.

"What, man? Nah, I told you I had to make a stop first so chill. What? Don't worry about it, man," he said. Natalia knew by the way he was talking that it was another woman on the other end. Usually that wouldn't bother her, but now that her feelings had gotten involved and their little arrangement was no longer what she wanted, she had a problem.

"Who is that, Qy?" she gave not one care if the woman on the other end heard her but obviously, Qyree did by how he turned to look at her.

Sucking her teeth, she got up and threw her robe back on and headed to the front of the house. Her little time with him was up and she was ready for him to leave if he didn't want to be there. Just as he was coming up the hall, there was a knock at her door. Rolling her eyes at him caused Qyree to laugh out loud which made her even madder.

Whoever it was, they were adamant about getting her attention. She knew that it wasn't any of her other sponsors because none of them knew where she lived, so she wasn't worried at all. Right as she opened the door, the woman on the other side was about to knock again.

"I know he didn't. Is Qyree here?" the woman said. Trinity couldn't believe that he had not only brought her to another woman's house but from the looks of it, he was in there giving away what she felt like was hers. Looking into the face of this mixed beauty, Trinity seethed on the inside. No matter how much she wanted to deny it, she had nothing on Natalia. Everything about her screamed dime while everything on Trinity couldn't even mumble nickel.

It wasn't like she was ugly or anything, but compared to the woman that had just been in there with her man, there was no candle on the face of the earth that she could hold to her.

Natalia gave her the once over and could tell she wasn't that much younger than her, but she was young enough so she better be his sister, while she was worried about if he was there or not. She wasn't even intimidated because by the look on the girl's face, she could already tell she was out of her league.

"Yeah, why?"

"Qyree!" she yelled, ignoring Natalia as Qyree appeared behind her. He had to make sure that he didn't leave anything of value there because as soon as he got the phone call and the knock on the door, he knew that it was about to go down. The last thing he wanted was to leave anything there that Natalia could destroy of his.

"Watch out, man," he said pushing Natalia to the side and walking out the door. "Didn't I tell you to wait in the car?"

"Yeah, and you also said this was your grandmama's house. She don't look like she drawing social security to me," Trinity said rolling her neck.

"This what we do now, Qyree? Bring these desperate chicks to my house while you lay up? Humph, that's real cute."

Looking at both of the women, he knew that they were probably thinking he was trying to get his lie together, but that couldn't have been farthest from the truth. He would have to actually care first before he did that. Neither of them, in his book, was good enough for an explanation so he gave none, as he walked down the driveway to his car.

Both ladies stood there stuck, not knowing what to say or do.

"Y'all gonna stay here and play sister wives or you getting on the road with me?"

"So this is why I couldn't go? 'Cause you taking this beauty supply store track wearing heffa with you?" Natalia was on a hundred and Qyree wasn't there for it. Although Natalia was putting on a front about going, she didn't really care because she had other plans for the weekend and they didn't involve Qyree.

Natalia was lost in her thoughts of what was to come and in that brief instance, Trinity used that to her advantage and caught her with a quick combo causing her to stumble back. Catching herself, Natalia got herself together and gave the girl what she was obviously in serious need of. A good ole southern behind whoopin!

Qyree laughed as he watched Trinity sneak Natalia, but she came back and started throwing bows. All he could do was shake his head at the sight. He didn't have time to play referee when he needed to get on the road. Reaching in the backseat, he grabbed Trinity's bags that she was taking with her, rolled down the window, and threw them out. She was so into getting her behind handed to her by Natalia that she didn't know that he was pulling off leaving her, until the bass dropped and Tory Lanez came through the speakers. He threw up the peace sign, as once again, Trinity was running behind his car screaming. Qyree didn't know why he was taking sand to the beach anyway, by taking her with him. Pulling out the blunt he had just rolled for the three-hour drive, he lit it up and headed towards the highway.

7

Jaxon walked out of his master bedroom down the hall to his wife's suite. It had been over ten years since the two slept in the same room, let alone the same bed. Zaria made it clear the last time she walked in on him in their marital bed, that it would be the last time she lay next to him. Instead of leaving like he thought she would, she moved all of her things out of their room and to the other end of the house. Zaria took her vows serious, but her belief in God even more serious, and felt like He would change Jaxon. Jaxon, on the other hand, didn't believe in all of that and felt like she would either continue to accept what he did or leave. Either decision she made would be fine with him.

Jaxon was overly arrogant and made no excuses for it. He was rich, owned a successful business, and looked good enough for the women to eat. He made sure to take care of himself and his body, and if there was a God, then He was making sure he got everything his heart desired. For that, he was thankful.

Not bothering to knock on the door, Jaxon walked right into his wife's room. Just like every other time he decided to see what she was up to, she was once again on her knees with her Bible open and her head bowed. That woman stayed on her knees but not for what he wanted her to, and that was exactly why he went elsewhere to get what he was lacking at home. There had been a time where Zaria would do whatever he asked her to do in their bed. Besides the fact that she was there with him before his career took off, her intimate skills were on point.

Sucking his teeth, he cleared his throat and waited for her to acknowledge him. After a few minutes of her not saying anything, he walked up closer behind her.

"I'm about to leave, Zaria," he said.

Still no response.

"Did you hear me?" he said louder this time, shaking her shoulder.

Instead of an audible response, what he got was a drunken moan as she leaned to the side and the Patrón bottle she was holding slipped from her hands and spilled on to the Bible.

"Looook wha juu mae me do Jax. Spillin' all my liquor!" Her eyes were bloodshot and she was sweating profusely as she tried to swing at him, causing her to lose her balance and fall back.

"I swear y'all Christians ain't no better than us sinners. The only thing y'all do is hide your sins behind the word of a God that you all think exist. In here getting drunk and still have the nerve to pray."

That was something that he couldn't understand about church folks and exactly why he didn't believe. They were always pointing their fingers at the ones who were open with their mess, but covered up their own. He couldn't and wouldn't respect them, nor would he serve their Master. They were all going to hell anyway if it existed, so why not go out with a bang?

"Don't ju go pointing fingers, missster. My God is an awesome God and He is a sovereign God. Yes He is! Glory to God!" she said throwing her head back and flailing her arms around in the air.

"Yea, whatever. I didn't come in here for all of that. I'm about to leave and head down to Valdosta and make sure my son is handling business," he told her, grabbing his suitcase handle.

"Humph no juur not. Juu don't care about jurr son let alone, buuuuuurrrrggg," she slurred before burping one of the loudest burps known to man. "Ooh chile, scuse me."

Jaxon looked on, shaking his head at her stumbling while trying to get up. He made no attempt to help her on the bed simply because she didn't need help getting in, in this state that she was in.

"How you figure I'm not going there to make sure he good?"

"Well for starters, you don't care nothing about that boy," she said finally making it to her destination. Jaxon observed her appearance and couldn't believe how bad she had let herself go. She was still beautiful, but the way she kept herself some days made him sick to his stomach.

"My son means more to me than you know. Why you think I'm still here after all of these years?" That statement must have gotten to her because she had sobered up real quick.

"Man, gone, 'cause you got some nerve! The only reason you are still here is because I allow it and you don't want me to take half of everything you own. I took care of our son while you were out there bed hopping! If you cared so much for him, you would have taught him how to be a real God fearing man, not some lowlife that likes to manipulate women to get between their legs." Zaria was on a rampage but this wasn't new to Jaxon. Whenever she drank, she got belligerent.

"Listen, if you had been taking care of home, I wouldn't have to get it elsewhere. And as for getting half of my money, that don't even matter. You'll be lucky to get any at all."

"If only you knew. You better believe one thing baby, your time is coming. Sooner than later, and you will reap what you sow."

"I don't have time for this. I got a three-hour drive," Jaxon said, turning his back to her so that he could walk out the door. What she said next was like a bomb dropping.

"Since when was Cancun a three-hour drive from here?" she asked.

How in the world did she know where he was going? Jaxon had always been the one to make sure to never put his escapades on any of his credit cards, although she knew he was unfaithful and his travel agent booked all trips.

"Mm hmm, that's right. Like I said, you reap what you sow. Oh, and before I forget. Since you are going to *Valdosta* so you say, to check on your son, make sure you let him know that you will be babysitting Natalia for him in Mexico," she dropped the epic bomb on him.

Not bothering to turn around and confirm nor deny the allegations, Jaxon simply walked out, leaving her to her drink herself into a coma. He didn't care that she knew about what he was doing, but the last thing he wanted to happen was for Qyree to find out his father was messing

around with one of his women.

8

"Hey boo!" Chey greeted, picking up the phone. It had been a few days since she had last spoken to Natalia and she was hoping that she was calling to tell her that she was on the way down. Von had talked her into having some fun and entering the talent showcase after she heard her singing at church. She felt like Chey's voice, along with the anointing she had, would be a breath of fresh air for the people. After a few days of turning her down, Cheynese finally agreed only to find out that she was already entered.

"Hey sis. Look, I have some bad news. Don't be mad at me but I won't be able to make the show. I know you're gonna kill it though," she said as she bit her lip on the other end of the phone. She knew that her girl was going to be upset but there was no way that she was going to miss out on a free all-expense paid trip.

"Come on Nat, why not? You know how I am about singing in front of people," she whined.

"Girl, stop. You do this at church with no problem."

"I know, but it's different. At church, I'm around other believers and they understand the message in what I sing. This is an event full of people who may not receive it."

"You got a point, but you know that God will never leave you nor forsake you, so no matter where you are as long as you are singing to the glory of Him, then He will work out the rest," Natalia encouraged.

Chey didn't know why Natalia had stopped going to church. Being that they both were raised up in the church, you would think that Natalia would continue to go hard for the Lord like she used to.

"I hear you."

"Don't sound like that. You know I'm right. Besides, if you kill it I'll bring you back something from Cancun," she teased.

"Ohhhh, now you know you not right for going without me!"

"I'll be back next week then we can hook up, I promise."

"Mm hmm, okay, we'll see. Have fun and be safe though," Chey said before ending the call.

Making sure she had her ID and cell phone, Chey got her car keys and headed out. If she was going to stop for gas and to pick Von up on the way to the school and be on time, she needed to leave ASAP.

Chey pulled up to the halfway house and sent a quick text to Von. She had to admit that she was extremely proud of the young lady. The two of them weren't too far in age from one another, so they were able to really click.

Getting to know her had been a real joy, and that made helping her get back on track with life even better. Jail may not have been the most favorable place for people, but instead of it being looked at as a bad thing, Von was using it to her advantage. She had even set a date to reunite with her son and it was coming up very soon.

Von: Here I come!

The text came through just before Von exited the house. Chey had to admit that even though it housed newly released inmates, it looked nothing like you would expect. The seven-bedroom house was beautiful. The lawn was always taken care of along with the flower bed at the foot of the porch, and the inside was just as nice. The Chief of Police was a wonderful woman of God who also attended church with Chey. It was her idea to make sure that when the women were released, they were released to a place where they would feel free and not still feel like they were caged animals.

Chief Warren made it clear that foolishness was not allowed, and if they got out of line they would be sent back. Often times when a prisoner went into one of those houses and the conditions of it still made it feel like they were behind bars, nothing would stop them from acting out. That's all they knew how to do. So this house that she affectionately named 'My Sister's Keeper' was available to help them to once again become a positive rehabilitated citizen. There were parenting classes for the ones who had lost their children in some way by going to jail, workshops for job searches, and tutoring for the ones that were determined to go back to school and may have needed some help. All in all, this was a blessing.

"Hey Ms. Broadus," she said, getting into the passenger seat.

"What I tell you about that?"

"I'm sorry. It's such a habit now," Von laughed. They made small talk as they pulled out of the driveway of the house. Chey made a left when she to the corner, and headed to the nearest gas station.

"You want anything out of here?" Von asked Chey.

"No thank you. My stomach is a ball of nerves and anything that goes down right now is sure to come back up." The was Chey was feeling about this performance had her nerves shot, and it felt like there were a million and one bats in her stomach instead of butterflies.

As Chey held on to the pump, a beautiful Benz pulled up on the other side of her. She didn't know too much about cars, but she could spot her dream car anywhere when she saw it. That was the one thing that she had always told herself she would get as a gift to herself before she left this world. Considering she had other priorities, that had to go on the backburner for now. She wasn't quite far enough in her career like she wanted to be to make that kind of purchase, but best believe with God on her side, she would one day.

Cheynese watched as the driver got out of the car, and immediately the smile on her face was so wide it caused her cheeks to hurt.

"Hey Qy," she said not wanting to seem too thirsty. The way he carried himself and the way the wind blew the scent of his cologne in her direction, had Chey in a daze.

"What's up beautiful?"

"Nothing. About to head over to your event. I was supposed to be going for moral support but somehow got bamboozled into performing."

"Oh word?" he said sounding excited but not too much. When Qyree was coming down the street, he noticed Cheynese standing next to her car. He didn't need gas, but he couldn't pass up the opportunity of being in her presence once again. He decided that when he got out he would act like he didn't see her, because he didn't want to seem too pressed about her.

His father had always taught him that there would never be a woman on the face of the earth that could give a man everything he needed to receive. That was why he should find more than one woman to satisfy those needs. The only thing they all had in common was that heavenly prize they held below the waist. Once upon a time, Jaxon thought that Zaria was going to be his all in all, but that quickly changed and so did his mindset about her.

"Yea, Von thought it would be a good idea to do it for fun. I didn't want to, but I finally gave in," she said shrugging her shoulders.

"And, she is about to sing them under too," Von said walking up behind them smiling.

"How you doing, love?" Qyree greeted.

"I'm good, how 'bout you?"

"Better, now that I hear Miss Lady is about to showcase her talent."

"Y'all better hope God decreases me and increases Himself on that stage 'cause if not, it's going to be a holy mess," Chey laughed.

"Nah, you got it. Well, let me head on over here to make sure everything and everybody are where they need to be. I'll see you in a bit."

"Okay."

Putting the nozzle back on the hook, both Cheynese and Von got into her car to head to the school. Before she pulled off, she glanced in the rearview mirror then over at Von.

"Why you looking at me like that?" Pure amusement was evident on Von's face but Chey didn't know why.

"That man got you open like a can of pig feet," Von laughed, sounding just like one of the twins in the movie *ATL*.

"He does not," she disagreed, hoping that Von would leave it alone. If she kept pressing her, she was going to eventually let it slip that she was in fact feeling Qyree. The only thing that kept him from being a prospect was his womanizing ways. He was far from a bad person, but boyfriend or husband material was not in him. Who was to say that it never would be, because God can surely change a person's heart and mindset, but Chey just wasn't about to be the one to put her heart on the line only for it to get broken.

"If you say so. I may have been out of the loop for a while but I know what it looks like when someone is feeling each other, and the two of y'all got it bad."

Chey couldn't deny that she liked him, just not enough to get misled. During their time in college, the rep Qyree had about him 'hitting it and quitting it' was warning enough she would never let him get close enough to hit and quit her. Or would he?

9

Getting to the event with only two hours left for the beginning of the show to start had Qyree stressed. He had wanted to be there earlier, but fooling around with Natalia and Trinity made him a little behind schedule. To some, he wasn't late but he knew better. Instead of getting right on the road the day before, he ended up leaving Natalia's house only to go to one of his other lady friend's houses. He was in serious need of a stress reliever and Bambi was the perfect one for that.

Bambi was a goddess. Her body was so flawless, but her attitude was horrible. He knew that if he went over to her house, there was no way that he could get what he wanted and leave right back out. After taking his stress away in the bed, as soon as he got up to leave she would stress him right back out by nagging and complaining. Heading her direction, he thought about just staying a few hours and then easing out on her. The gag was on him when he woke up and the sun was out. Since she knew he had an event in Valdosta, she didn't complain as much. Now here he was trying to make sure he didn't miss anything that needed to be done.

Things were going just as he had hoped for and the only thing that would be better was if he could sign a few cats that he was sure to bring in millions. By the time his father got back from vacation with one of his lady friends, the contracts would be on his desk, signed, sealed, and delivered.

It was odd that at the last minute, Jaxon told him he wouldn't be able to make it. When asked who he was going with, Jaxon only said a 'friend' which was unusual to Qyree. He knew all of the women that his father went on trips with and for him not to offer up any more info, Qyree let it go. Sooner or later he would meet her just like he met all the other ones, so he didn't sweat it.

The booing of the crowd broke him away from his thoughts, as he watched the performer leave the stage. It was some dude that got up there thinking he was Prince of the new millennium with the outfit to match. He wore his hair in a big afro and the bell-bottom outfit he was rocking was definitely not a crowd pleaser. They were so ruthless with their pettiness, Qyree could have sworn he ran off with tears in his eyes. He knew better.

Fallon, one of the girls Qyree had hired to be the emcee for the night, was coming out looking like she wanted to laugh but was fighting hard not to.

"Now y'all know y'all wrong for that," she giggled before introducing the next act. "Coming straight from Waycross Georgia, this man is about to let y'all know that Christians can get turnt up too! Please welcome to the stage, Mike Murk!"

Qyree had been looking for this performance ever since his father's assistant dropped his name. He thought it would be good to have him put on a little concert and although he was still unsigned, they still made sure to lace his pockets for blessing them. He heard dude had really been poppin' down that way and the crowd was getting too hype. Qyree's father let him know that Mike was in the works with a major record label already, so he wasn't going to step on anyone else's toes. Believe it or not, the music industry was small when you were on the inside, and he was pretty sure that had he made a move to sign Mike, it would spell trouble for Hype Lyfe. He was making a name for himself in the Christian community and had the potential to help them break out into another genre. They didn't have any gospel rappers or singers and this was an area they could really tap into.

Qyree thought about when he would go to church with his mother back in the day and the songs they would sing would bore him to death. That was one of the reasons he had stopped going long ago. He couldn't relate to anything that was being sung or preached.

Mike was a tall dark-skinned guy, with glasses that gave him the intellectual look, and his swag was on ten. There was something about him that stood out to Qyree other than the fact that he was in music. Like, God had his hand on him or something.

The kids that he brought out on the stage with him looked to be no older than fourteen years old. There were three girls and two boys who had looks on their faces like they were about to kill whatever it was they were to do. Qyree assumed it was to dance and he couldn't wait to see what this was all about. Everybody in the audience was getting excited as they watched the two teen boys, one with a hairstyle that resembled the cut Odell Beckham, Jr. rocked and was dyed red, and the other wearing a bomb bucket hat. On cue, the pair began getting them hype.

Qyree could tell they had to be brothers because they were so in sync with one another. The music began and it was on!

"Dealing with so much but I never fail, devil wanna see me go on my way to hell. Don't invest any stress on me, I don't want it at all. No time for the mess I don't struggle with the rest oh no baby I don't fall. I stand on my own two feet head being held up high. Worried 'bout nothing you can see I'm good got a smile on my face everywhere I'm fly."

The beat was so sick that Qyree couldn't believe that Mike had written and composed the whole thing. His father's assistant had done research on him and found that out. He was bound to blow up with that type of capability. Qyree wanted to kick himself when he let his father talk him out of reaching out when he first wanted to.

By the time the chorus came in, Qyree found himself dabbin' and Milly rockin' while singing along with everybody else.

"Won't let no one come and steal my joy, 'cause I got God wit me. AW YEAH! Won't take no mess comin' from you, boy, cause I got God wit me. AW YEAH! Won't let no scamboogers steal my peace, 'cause I got God wit me. AW YEAH! I'm not at war but I'm still at peace, 'cause I got God wit me!"

He did a few more songs and each one got better and better as they went along. He even did one called "Better" where he performed with some dude who was nice with the vocals. Qyree loved him some old school rap and thought that no one could ever top the late great Nate Dogg and Warren G, but those two proved him wrong. He knew one thing, if that record label didn't sign Mike Murk, Hype Lyfe Records was going to. His father would just have to get on board.

Qyree made a mental note to go check out his

REVERBNATION page and see if he had any new

material. Mike Murk was about to be a household name

and there would be no stopping him once he got on.

10

Lord, have mercy... how am I going to go after that? Chey thought to herself. She wouldn't dare say it out loud because she knew that Von would have something to say and backing out at the last minute was not an option.

Rubbing her sweaty palms on the front of her romper, she did her best to calm herself.

"Girl, you will be just fine. You see Mike Murk just set the atmosphere and how well they received him. You good, boo," Von encouraged.

Now that was something she could agree with. That performance was awesome. She had even peeped Qyree out there going in with everyone else. Just as she was feeling herself starting to gain control of her emotions, she heard the announcer call her name. It was show time and God was needed front and center.

Applause erupted and she was so glad that she decided to wear some cute little Toms shoes instead of her original pair of stilettos she normally wore with that outfit. Her legs were so wobbly, there was no doubt that she would have been on her face right now. Taking in and releasing the breath she was holding, she made her way to the mic.

Von smiled at her friend because that was exactly what Chey had been to her since her release. She knew the day that she walked into her probation office that Chey was as pure as they came. Chey reminded her so much of her friend Nivea that she thought God was giving her another chance at having a real friendship in another person.

So many nights after God had touched her heart about what she had done to Nivea, Von lay in her bunk crying because she realized just how bad she had hurt that girl. Because of her selfishness and loyalty to her mother, Von had lost one of the most important people in her life at the time. She thought she would never forgive herself for having been the one to set Nivea up to be raped. That one incident was the beginning of so many lives being destroyed, hers included.

God truly worked in mysterious ways and would turn a situation around in the blink of an eye. Good or bad, He could do it and He did. Von knew that everything that God did was already preordained before the creation of the earth, so He knew what would happen. So many times she wished He had given her a sneak peek into it all, but she knew that wouldn't have allowed the growth that was needed in everybody involved. Things in life could hurt so bad at times, but she learned that there was purpose in the pain that we rarely saw.

Nivea was covered and favored by God like Abel was. She was the apple of everyone's eye the minute she walked into their lives. It wasn't forced, it was just who she was as a person. Von was so jealous, like Cain, that she couldn't see that it was God's doing and not the works of Nivea. While she tried to bring harm to Nivea, the harm fell on her instead.

Von shook her head at the memories but thanked God that she was finally healed, delivered, and set free from that pain. The devil held her mistakes over her head for so long, but no more would he be able to and she had Nivea to thank for that. Wasn't it funny that some of the same people that we hurt would be the same ones that would also help us heal? You burned the bridge but they trusted God enough to build another one and help you back across. Nobody but God was capable of changing a heart like that. He was definitely worthy.

11

If they weren't outside, Cheynese was pretty sure that the attendees would hear her knees knocking and her teeth chattering. Her nerves were beyond shot. They were dead and in their grave. Why hasn't God jumped in yet? She knew He was there 'cause He was the one that decided to be omnipresent in everything. Jesus come through! Just as she was about to run off and hide under a rock, her eyes locked with Qyree and he gave her a reassuring smile. That one gesture eased her fears and she was ready.

"I know that this is a different type of atmosphere, but I want all of you under the sound of my voice to just begin to give God some praise. You don't have to know the Bible from cover to cover in order to worship Him. There is no hurt too painful for Him to heal. Open your mouths and hearts to receive," Chey began, just as the track for Jekalyn Carr's "Greater Is Coming" began to blow through the speakers. "That's it right there. See, if it had not been for God I wouldn't be standing here today. Years ago the enemy wanted to take me out of here, but God pressed upon my heart that my greater is coming."

All of the worry and anxiousness that Chey felt since she agreed to do this was now gone. Looking out into the faces of the people that stood before her let her know that God was controlling this and He would get the glory out of it. Once again, her eyes landed on Qyree as she said, "No matter how far out of God's will you think you may be, God's grace and mercy are sufficient enough to draw you back to Him."

Chey hadn't even started singing yet and Von was already in tears, with her arms raised above her head, sending up her worship.

"If it had not been for the shaking, I never woulda been ready for the making," she began singing. The look of pure amazement was evident in every face, especially Qyree's, as he watched and listened. The chills he got were nothing like he had ever experienced. Looking down at his arms, he saw the many tiny goosebumps that were revealing themselves in almost hundred-degree weather.

"That's it, daughter. Come get your breakthrough. I feel a breaking in the spirit preparing me for greater. He hears your heart son. Greater is coming. Step out on faith and receive it. Greater is coming. Hold on 'cause greater is coming. Hold on to that promise that He made sis. It's coming, my greater is coming! Yes it is! Just hold on and receive," Chey encouraged some of the people around her and that was when she understood God's purpose for her being there.

"He's preparing you. Walk into your greater. Have your way God. Do it in this place for your people," she continued even after the song was over. It took a good twenty minutes to a half an hour to finally have people able to get up from where they had fallen or sat while they were in worship. God let His anointing fall fresh as He restored and brought back home His children who had strayed.

12

"I'm so proud of you," Von told Chey as she made her way to the back. It had been a long time since either of them had felt this type of power, and they knew that the only source it could come from was God. All you had to do to experience him was move out of His way and let Him take the lead.

"Girl, that was nobody but God. I was too close to running off stage but at the last possible moment, He showed up. I haven't felt like this in a long time," she smiled.

"Well, I know He is well pleased. Why do you only sing in church? Your voice is so anointed you could give quite a few artists a run for their money in the industry," Von stated. The look of sadness that immediately washed over Chey's face didn't go unnoticed.

"What's wrong?" she asked, while preventing Chey to move any further.

Not wanting to go back to that horrible time, Chey told her only what she wanted her to know right then. It had been a long time since that incident, but still not long enough to go into detail.

"I haven't been in the studio in years. I put my career at the top of my list so I kinda let that part of my life go," she half told the truth. Chey loved being in the studio years ago because that was where she found her relief. Singing unto the glory of the Lord was like therapy for her. Then one day it was all snatched away and she never went back to reclaim it.

"You sung professionally?" they heard coming from behind them. Turning around to where the voice had come from, they saw Qyree.

"No, not professionally. I wanted to, but you know how our plans aren't always what God has in mind for us and we have to merge into the lane that He wants us in. I guess that wasn't my lane," she laughed a laugh of sadness. Both Qyree and Von could tell that her heart was in singing just by her performance alone.

"Yo, you should really get back in there. The world needs that voice you have been gifted with," Qyree encouraged. Watching her on that stage and how she ministered to the young crowd was amazing to him. He saw eyes being opened, lives being changed, and hearts being healed while she sang. It wasn't forced. It was authentic and real and he could tell that she was in the wrong career field.

Before she had a chance to respond to him, a pretty dark-skinned girl walked up behind him with two of her friends. She was beautiful with her long curly hair and bright eyes, but the smug look and the way she looked

Cheynese up and down instantly turned her ugly. Chey didn't understand why women acted like that towards other women they didn't even know. She chalked it up to some kind of insecurities they must have had because that was the only way she could see them having an issue with her. They knew nothing about her and from the way they were acting, she wasn't interested in letting them into her world anyway.

"Bae, how you gonna tell me and my girls to drop by so you can show us a good time but then you in the next broad's face," she said, once again, looking at Von and Chey crazy. Home girl obviously thought she was going to get a reaction out of her, but was sadly mistaken. She did get a response but not what she thought or from who she thought.

"Aye shawty, look. First of all, you not the only female I invited, ask your girl right there. I bet she didn't tell you that. Second, we not even that cool for you to be calling me bae. I ain't even hit yet and you already catching feelings. And last, who I talk to is none of your concern. I don't even know why I just explained anything to you fo' real," Qyree said shocking everybody. "I'll get up with you later Chey, and again, you did an amazing job.

"Okay, and thank you. I'm so glad you liked it," she told him, unbothered by the women who had just been put in their place.

Qyree returned his attention back to the three women. "So you coming with me or nah? I ain't got time to be playing games."

For a minute, Chey thought the girl that had just gotten her face cracked was about to bow out gracefully. There was no way she was going to let him talk to her like that and still leave with him. The girl stood there contemplating if she wanted to go because of the way he just played her, but thought against it. If she played his little game and went along with him, she was sure that what she had to offer him would have him coming back for more. That meant the more he came back the more money he would drop in her hands. Qyree was loaded and almost everyone knew it.

"You right, Qy. My bad. You know I'm going with you," she said batting her eyes at him.

"Typical," Von scoffed and sucked her teeth, and Chey elbowed her in her side to make her stop.

"Excuse me?" one of the other women said coming to the ringleader's defense. Von turned her head from side to side then craned her neck to look behind her.

"Von, what are you doing?" Chey asked. Now Chey was far from being a punk. As a matter of fact, back in her day, she wouldn't hesitate putting her hands to work. Now that she was older and had a career, her character and reputation were important to her and she wouldn't dare let anyone bring her down to their level. They could say what they wanted about her walking away from a negative situation all they wanted to, but at the end of the day, the approval of God was the only one she cared about.

"I'm trying to figure out who this sock puppet is talking to," Von said causing Chey's mouth to drop open and tears began forming in her eyes. She wasn't getting teary eyed because she was sad, but because her inside was screaming in laughter and she was trying not to let it come out.

Chey couldn't lie though, the girl looked just like a sock with drawn on facial features. Anybody that saw her could tell that those St. Louis arches she had drawn on her forehead was not life, and she looked flat out foolish. If it was to pour down raining at that very moment she would be in trouble.

"Sock puppet? I know you didn't with those thrift store clothes on. You could never get on my level, honey," the girl called herself clapping back.

"You're right, boo. I can't see myself walking around in those HuaNOTches. So if that's what it's like to be on your level, stop the elevator now cause I caaaaan't," Von clowned. This time Chey couldn't hold it in. The fact that Von had just told that girl she had on fake Huaraches and looked like a sock puppet had her dead and waiting on Jesus to accept her in. That last comment must have made her realize she was no match for Von, so she cut her losses and walked off, pulling the girl who had remained quiet the whole time.

"I'll catch up with you later," Qyree told Chey and walked off, trying not to laugh out loud. He didn't know who Von was to Chey, but whoever she was he could tell that she would make sure to protect Chey at all cost.

13

"You not coming in?" Fatima asked with the car door open. Her two girls Naja and Drea had already gotten out and was headed towards the front door of her apartment. They already knew what was about to go down and they couldn't wait.

When Fatima told them she had bumped into the well-known Qyree Reeves and he had asked her to meet him with some friends so they could get it poppin', all they saw were dollar signs. Naja didn't say a word when Fatima made her announcement, because he had asked her too. Her hopes were that once he was finished with the other two, he would slide off with her alone. In order to do that, they couldn't know. She just had no idea that Qyree would put her on blast like that in front of everybody. There was no way that Tima was going to let her be alone with him and miss out on her meal ticket. They were all ready for a come up.

"Nah, I'm straight. I need to head back to the city. I got some stuff I need to handle," he said not giving her too much attention. His mind was so preoccupied with thoughts of Cheynese that he couldn't think straight. He needed to get somewhere and just think and he couldn't do that around those three who were only out to try and win his affection with their bodies. Under normal circumstances he would be all for it. Nothing like hitting and dipping and on to the next, but tonight it just wasn't in him. Something was pulling at him and he didn't know what.

"You got some *stuff* to handle or *somebody*?" Fatima sassed yet again. If she hadn't worn her welcome out before with that first stunt she tried to pull in front of Chey, she had surely done it now.

Snapping his head in her direction, he looked her over before speaking. Fatima was stacked and she was also beautiful, but her attitude stunk. He had dealt with women with bad attitudes before, more often than not, but it was something about her attitude that was a big turn off.

"Yo, didn't I tell you already not to question me? Who or what I do does not concern you. What part of that don't you understand? You're not my woman and never will be," he said, once again crashing her face. But Fatima couldn't let him leave.

Fatima had planned it out perfectly when she knew the talent search was coming to the city. She did everything she could to wind up in the path of Qyree so that she could get him to notice her, and it was just her luck that he came through the drive-thru of her job one day. When he asked for her number and told her he wanted to get up with her after the show, she was ready to take her headset off right then and tell Mr. Burney she quit! If she could bed Qy, she would be set for life. All of her attempts before of getting

pregnant by a baller had failed, so tonight was a must. She

was tired of living from paycheck to paycheck so she had

to do something quick to get him to stay.

"I'm sorry, boo. I don't know why I be trippin' so

bad. Maybe it's because I feel such a strong connection and

I know it can't be a coincidence that we ran into one

another. Come on in so we can make you feel better," she

crooned.

Watching the lies spill out of her mouth, Qyree

wore a smug look on his face. Fatima was trying her best to

get him in there and he knew why. She was a trapper. Not

trapper as in dealing with drugs, but a woman whose sole

purpose was to come up by trapping a man with a baby.

Qyree may have been a lot of things but a fool he was not.

He could see it all in her eyes and he was ready to get far

away from her as possible. He already had a little situation that he was dealing with in the baby area, and he didn't need it again.

"Get out shawty," he simply stated.

"Don't be like that, baby. Let me make you feel good. I can send Naja and Drea home and it can be just me and you."

Looking blankly into her face she finally got the picture and got out with much attitude. Qyree watched her throw her hips to the side extra hard in hopes that it would change his mind, and it almost did. Mama was working with something and she knew it, it just wasn't worth it.

Pulling out his phone, he started smiling immediately at what he was about to do.

Qyree: U tryna slide off wit a G?

912-555-6363: I thought u were chillin tonight.

Qyree: Nah

912-555-6363: Aight

Qyree knew it was about to be some mess, as he put his car into reverse just as Naja came out of the house. Fatima and Drea weren't far behind her yelling, and all he could do was laugh. He knew as soon as Fatima had showed out in front of Chey, he was gonna move to the next with Naja. She proved that she was worthy of a few minutes of alone time because she kept her mouth closed about him wanting to meet up with her too. Had it been the other way around, Fatima would have told the world.

Not paying any attention to the yelling and screaming, he headed to the nearest hotel. He just needed something to relax him before he headed home.

***

Traffic was to a minimum as Qyree rode down the interstate. He was so deep in his thoughts that the time seemed to fly by faster than normal. Turning the volume up on his sound system, he tried to let the noise drown out his thoughts but it was to no avail. Before he knew it, he was pulling up to his parents' estate and just sat there. He was a grown man living at his parents' house. Not because he couldn't afford to leave, it was just that he didn't have a reason to. They let him stay there rent free, come and go as he pleased, and was able to either stack his money or splurge on anything he wanted.

In the last year, he had bought 3 brand new, off the lot luxury cars, just because. He didn't need them but it just seemed to do something to his ego when he got praise everywhere he went in either of them. People wanting to take pictures of them just to post to their social media pages and he let them. It was even better when the people recognized who he was when they saw him. His mother told him that all of that would get old to him one day. The women, cars, blowing money, and not having a relationship with God. She saw so much more potential in him than he saw in himself. All he saw was him being young and rich and taking over one of the biggest record companies in the nation, but his mother saw past all of that. She saw what God saw, and prayed fervently that one day his own eyes would be open.

"Ma! Where you at?" he yelled walking into the house. He threw his keys on the table beside the door and dropped his overnight bag on the floor. In that moment, he didn't know why he had even bothered to take an overnight bag because he didn't stay overnight.

The whole ride to the hotel, Naja talked his ear off and was asking question after question. The conversation had no depth to it and for the first time, Qyree noticed that. He had never been the one to care if a conversation was deep or not between him and a woman. It simply didn't matter. All he needed was to get to that heavenly place and chuck up the deuces once he was done. Since the first day he had ran back into Chey on the campus all the way up until that very moment, she had been on his mind like no other woman had. Because of that, when he pulled up to the hotel and checked in, he gave Naja the key, told her to go on up and he would meet her, and he got in his car and left. She blew his phone up with text after text and voicemail after voicemail, until he finally got tired of it and blocked her number as he headed home.

"You're back early. How did everything go?" his mother said coming around the corner. There was something different about her than before he left. Her eyes were clear and twinkling, but there was something else in them that he couldn't figure out what it was. She had obviously pulled herself together but it was out of her character. Instead of touching on that right then, he filled her in.

"Yea, I wasn't trying to stay down there until tomorrow. But the show went better than I expected. I signed this male and female R&B duo and another rapper who I know will put me in line to be Senior A&R of the company," he said but his voice lacked excitement. This had been one of his lifelong dreams as far as he could remember, so to see him not the least bit amped was out of character.

"Aren't you happy? This is what you have been wanting for the longest," she said walking over to him and ushering him into the living room for them to sit.

"Yes and no. I mean, yes, because it's my dream but no, because even if I get it, who besides you will share in this moment with me?" he told her and she immediately knew what he was thinking.

For so many years she had heard her husband teach their son that he didn't need one woman in his life, he needed many. Although it hurt her, she had no one to blame but herself because she stayed and allowed it. All Zaria wanted was for her son to grow up with both of his parents when she found out she was pregnant with him. It was before Jaxon had started being flat out disrespectful with his indiscretions, and once it hit the fan that she felt like it was too late for her. But at that moment, she felt like God was answering her prayers by speaking to her son's heart.

"So what else happened at the show?" Zaria asked and his face began to light up. There had to be a woman involved but right now wasn't the time for her to ask him. She would just wait until he was ready to spill the beans.

"Awww man, Ma, let me tell you who I ran into," he said, getting hyped. "Remember that time you and Dad came out to Cali to visit me at school and I introduced you to my tutor named—"

"Cheynese," his mother finished for him, throwing him for a loop. How in the world did she know he was talking about her and better yet, how could she remember her off the top of her head like that? He knew that he had asked if she remembered, but he had planned on her telling him no and he would have to jog her memory.

"I remember her like I met her thirty seconds ago," she smiled.

Looking at his mother he was at a loss for words until she spoke again.

"What about her?"

"I saw her before the show when I was finalizing everything at the school. We chopped it up for a few and then she left. Well, when I got there and got a list of who the performers were that had entered the contest, her name was on there. Ma, when I tell you that she has the voice of an angel..." he trailed off. Zaria watched him as he sat back in a daze, with a look of admiration on his face as he thought of Chey.

Zaria could never forget the girl as long as she lived. The moment she met her all of those years ago, she knew the girl was something special. Everything about her was pure and she had hoped that one day her son would call to tell her that they were a couple, but that day never came. He was too much like his father to settle down and that saddened her. As bad as she wanted Qyree to settle down with the girl that she had only met for a few minutes, she was glad that he didn't pursue her. The last thing Zaria wanted was for Chey was to have her heart snatched from her chest the same way Jaxon continued to do hers.

"I didn't know she was a singer. I thought she said she was in school for Criminal Justice," Zaria remembered. Qyree looked over at his mother as she had a questioning look on her face.

"Ma, how you remembering all of this stuff about her and you only talked to her for a few minutes?" he asked.

Smiling, she said, "Baby, you never forget a person who is after God's own heart. It's just something in them that makes it hard to forget. I could tell in just that small amount of time that she was special."

He couldn't argue with her on that one. He, too, had felt it the first time he laid eyes on her when he walked into the student library.

Qyree couldn't believe that he was on the verge of failing a subject his first semester. He couldn't blame anyone but himself though, because he partied more than he studied and the different girls in and out of his dorm room didn't help either. Qyree knew that he could pass on his own had he just applied himself and been in class like he was supposed to be, but he was about to enjoy the college life and all it had to offer. The only reason he allowed his professor to set his up a tutor was because he didn't want to hear his parents' mouth when they came to visit in a few months. He knew as soon as they touched down they were going to be snooping around. Because he was well known just by who his father was, there was no way that he could embarrass them by flunking out of school.

Walking into the library, Qyree looked for a girl fitting the description he was given. Scanning the room, his eyes finally fell on the back of her head. From the angle he was looking from, he could see she was wearing a fitted jean shirt with the sleeves rolled up to her elbows, a pair of dark jean capris, and some low top Converse. Her long hair was almost down her back and it was pulled behind her ear. She wore a pair of thin framed eye glasses on her face. He couldn't see her full face, but from the little he saw, he knew she was beautiful.

Walking over to the table she was sitting at with a pen to her lips, with her right hand and her left hand massaging her scalp, she looked like she was deep in thought and couldn't find whatever she was looking for in the textbook in front of her.

"Excuse me, are you Chey? I hope I'm pronouncing it right," he said.

"Hi," she smiled up at him and at that moment, he thought he was going to pass out. It wasn't because she looked like all of the girls he chased after, but because she didn't look like them. She held such an innocence about her and seeing her face completely let him know the side view didn't do her justice. The girl was gorgeous.

"It's actually pronounced like Chi not Shay," she said. He was glad that she wasn't offended that he called her the wrong name.

Sitting across from her as he put his backpack on the table, he began to take out the thing he needed for the study session.

"My fault. So Chey, is that a nickname or your full name?" he asked her.

"It's short for Cheynese," she said and waited. She knew the response that she was about to get and she laughed on the inside. It was always the same whenever she told anyone her real name.

"You mean like the food and the country?" he said causing her to double over in laughter. Even the sound of her voice and the laughter she let out was beautiful.

"I see now why you need a tutor. Yes, like the food, but Chinese is not a country," she smiled, making him embarrassed. He had never been around a woman that made him act the way that he had in that moment, and he was thrown off. Qyree couldn't believe that he had just said something so stupid in front of her.

"You got jokes, huh?" he said trying to redeem himself. He couldn't stop looking at her and after a few

moments of an intense stare down, they got going on the material they needed to go over.

Almost an hour into their session, they had hit it off. Not only was she helping him catch up on his work, but he was enjoying her company. He had yet to tell her who his father was and she didn't seem to know right away like the other females on campus. The more he talked to her, the more he liked being around her. That was until she brought up a topic of discussion that made him uncomfortable. God.

All he could think about as she sat there talking about her life as a preacher's kid and doing ministry, was hoping his session would be over. He didn't want to be rude and cut her off, so he made like he was paying attention. He may not have listened to the words she was saying, but he saw the joy that she had plastered on her face. Whatever she was saying, he could tell made her happier than anything.

"So this what you do? Can't answer my call but you in here with the next chick," the girl that came out of thin air said. Neither Chey nor Qyree saw her coming in since they were both in their own thoughts. Had he seen her, he would have made sure to turn in the other direction. Tameika was a stalker to him and he didn't know how to get rid of her. She was the type that once she got out of your bed, she thought she was in a relationship. No matter how good her body felt to him, she just couldn't offer him anything else. In all honesty, no woman could. All he needed was her body.

"Well, I guess our session is over. I'll see you tomorrow at the same time," Chey said gathering her things and walking off, not waiting on him to confirm. What impressed him the most though was how she totally ignored Tameika. Every time he was with someone new and would see one of the other women he was messing with, they always ended up in a yelling match or actually fighting,

while he stood back and laughed. To see grown women fighting over him did nothing but feed his ego and he couldn't wait to tell his father all about it.

"You wild, yo," he said getting his stuff up and looked at her. Tameika had a nice body but her face and attitude were as ugly as they came. He didn't know why she thought he would have her on his arm on the regular 'cause she was only good behind closed doors and with the lights off. Ignoring the words that were coming out of her mouth, just like he had done Chey when she got on her "God wagon", he headed out the door.

The more time he spent with Chey while she helped him with his class, the closer he felt to her, but she was pulling away. She was strictly on the friend tip and after a while, he wasn't pressed for her. There was a campus full of ready and willing women to assist him with what he wanted. He was completely over trying to get with Chey.

14

After going back down memory lane, Qyree filled
his mother in on everything with the show. He could tell by
the way she was looking at him that she was proud of the
decision he had made concerning the direction of the
company, but she was also worried that Jaxon wouldn't go
along with it. It was a step in a direction that she knew he
wouldn't want to go in. She was definitely going to need
her prayer warriors to intercede for her child. He was going
to need it.

"Zaria!" Jaxon yelled out coming through the front
door.

"In here," she said sitting back on the couch,
waiting for him to enter.

"What's good son? How did everything go? You
got something for me?" Jaxon rattled off. Qyree knew that

he was referring to signing someone and by the big smile that slid across his face, Jaxon already knew what was up.

"You already know how I do," Qyree said feeling himself. He knew that after all of the hard work he was putting in, there would be no doubt in his mind who would land in that top spot.

"Absolutely. With the talent you just found I know my new partner is going to be able to bring in more artists being our head A&R," he said knocking the wind out of both Qyree and his mother.

"What!" they yelled at the same time while Jaxon stood there looking confused.

"What's wrong with the two of you?" he asked.

"How you going to give the position that I been busting my behind for since I can remember, to someone else? Who else can or had been bringing it like I have for this company?" Qyree was furious. All of the years and the hard work that he had put in to secure his spot, and here his father was trying to give it away.

His father may not have said who he was putting in that spot, but he already had an idea that it was his right hand man, Reginald. He understood that his father and Reginald were best friends since the sandbox, but he was his heir, his first born, his only son. If it wasn't for Qyree, they wouldn't have the new artists that he had signed who were bringing in the majority of the money. All of the people that Reginald had signed flopped, so how his father wanted him to represent them was beyond him.

"First of all, you are going to respect me in my house and lower your voice. I'm not one of these jump-offs that you can talk to. You better check yourself," Jaxon said walking over to him.

Qyree had never disrespected his father in all of the years he had been on the face of this earth, but today was a new day. He wasn't about to let someone take something he worked for right from under him.

"Yo Dad, on the real, fall back. I've never disrespected you but I'm a grown man and you standing in my personal space," Qyree said holding his own as Zaria was holding her breath. She didn't know what was about to go on and there was no way that she was about to answer the door to whoever it was that was on the other side, ringing it like they were crazy. She didn't know what would happen if she left the two of them alone.

"Second," Jaxon began like Qyree didn't just open his mouth and moved closer to his face. "What I do with my company is my business. I started this from the ground up and just because you think you poppin' for signing a few acts, don't forget who brought you in. If it wasn't for me you wouldn't be where you are today," Jaxon said grilling his son. He knew that Qyree had been waiting and working for that top spot, but he wasn't about to let him get that high up in rank. Of course he loved his son, but he loved his money and lifestyle more. As good as Qyree was, there was no doubt in his mind that his son would supersede him and pass him by. That wasn't something that he was willing to let happen. Jaxon wasn't about to let someone else take the shine off of him, even if it was his own son.

Looking his father up and down one last time, Qyree walked over to the door because the ringing of the bell was annoying him about just as much as his father's revelation. Whoever it was needed to come back later. Now was not the time. He wasn't sure who it was but he knew they were mad. Between the ringing of the bell, the pounding on the door, he knew they were adamant about getting in. It didn't dawn on him right then that the security gate didn't call to the house to inform them of a guest. So that meant whoever it was, was already on their property.

Flinging the door open with a scowl on his face, it dropped at the sight of Natalia.

***

It felt like everything in Qyree's life was falling apart and he had no clue where to go to start piecing things back together. Everything he had been working so hard for had been snatched away concerning his career, and if that wasn't bad enough he found out that his father's secret mistress that he didn't know about was the same woman he was messing with. It wasn't like he was going to pop the question to Natalia, but to find out what she was up to and all of her secrets wasn't cool. He figured the least she could do was be straight up with him since he had never hidden anything from her. She knew that there were other women and in the beginning, she was cool, but when her feelings got involved, then all of a sudden he was supposed to line up with her. If Qyree wasn't lining up with the word of

God, he didn't know why she would expect him to do it with her.

As soon as he saw her standing on the porch of his parents' house he knew it was time for him to leave. He hopped in his car and left the screaming behind him as he mashed out of the driveway, with no intended final destination. Qyree had driven for so long with his mind boggled that he didn't realize he had made it to Valdosta until he pulled up to the college. It was almost 8pm and not a soul was in sight. Not even 24 hours ago he was just there and here he was being led back but didn't know why.

Who was he kidding? He knew exactly why he ended up back there and her name was Cheynese. As bad as he wanted to fight it, old feelings that he thought he had buried were slowly rising to the surface again. The very first time he met her, something in him was sparked, and just as he was about to make his move, one of his side joints broke that up. For the remainder of the time Chey tutored him, it was strictly business. She made it her business not to let anything grow between them except a friendship, and if that was all that she would give then he was cool with that.

Whenever he saw her on campus, she was always smiling, friendly to others, and being a help wherever it was needed. But what stood out to him the most was the fact that no one ever mentioned her sleeping around with different dudes like the majority of the girls in school. He couldn't remember a time where any of his boys heard rumors about her, and she never associated herself with a bunch of catty females. He didn't know what kind of material God cut her from but she was definitely cut from a different cloth from everybody else. Had he not been so jacked up in the head by the teachings of his father, he probably would have pursued her. Who knows where they would be today.

After sitting for a few minutes in the parking lot, he decided to go grab himself something to eat and cop him a room for a few days. He didn't know how long he was going to be there, but he knew he needed to be away from Atlanta for a while.

Once he got situated in his suite, had eaten, and taken a shower, he got in the plush bed with one hand resting behind his head in deep thought. Something had changed in him but he couldn't quite place it. All he knew was that he needed to see Chey. The way she sang and worshipped on that stage, took him to another place.

Qyree picked up his phone to shoot her a text and remembered that he forgot to get her number. So much had been going on that it had slipped his mind. He wondered if she would even give it to him, but he was going to try anyway. He didn't talk to her long enough to find out where she was working and he was almost out of ideas until it dawned on him, Facebook. Everyone had a page these days, all the way down to kids, so he was sure to find her on there.

It took him a few minutes to remember her last name and prayed that she hadn't gotten married and changed it. He didn't notice a ring or tan line on her ring finger, but that didn't mean that she was still married. Divorce was an option. He knew there was no one else on the face of the earth that had her name, but Qyree didn't even know how to spell it.

After about twenty minutes of searching, he was about to give up when one of their college classmates popped up on his screen. His last hope was that the two of the women were friends and he could find her that way. He was so anxious to find out and was getting irritated going through the thousands of friends on the list, until there she was.

She wasn't online at the time, but he had hoped that she would see the message fairly quick. Right then, he felt like the only one that could bring him some type of comfort was Chey. Zaria had been telling him all of his life that when he needs comfort, God was his main source. Since Qyree hadn't talked to the man upstairs in so long, Chey had to be the next best thing. He was sure that she would listen. He wasn't so sure if God would.

All he said to her was that he needed to see her. Scrolling down his timeline for another hour or so, he noticed all of the females that he had either run through over time, or ones he wanted to smash before. But now it was like he was disgusted by what he saw, and it was starting to not be appealing to him anymore. What on earth was going on with him? Not having the energy to even want to figure it out, he turned his phone off and shut his eyes as he let sleep find him immediately.

15

Chey watched as Von continued to be fighting to sit still. They were waiting at Chey's house because this was the day that Von would be reunited with her son, Amir. After so many years behind bars, she was finally going to be able to have her baby back in her life.

"Von, honey, you have to calm down," she said walking over to the window where she was pacing.

"I know, but I can't. What if he doesn't want anything to do with me? I don't know if I can take that kind of pain," Von said as a lone tear fell from her eye.

Wiping it away from her face with her thumb, Chey closed her eyes and began to pray. By the time she was done, she could feel the tension leave Von's body little by little.

"God's perfect will is going to be done. Whatever that is, I promise you will have peace," she smiled at her friend.

She had no idea what Von was feeling because she had never been in that kind of situation, so all she could do was encourage her the best way that she could at the moment. Chey had briefly spoken to Nivea, the one who was raising Von's son, and who was also the woman that Von set up to be raped. Even with the little time they talked on the phone, Chey could tell she was a beautiful spirit and although she had been deeply hurt, her love for God took away all of that inability to forgive that she was holding on to. If it wasn't for Him, there would be no way that she would be able to face Von again, let alone raise her child.

Hearing the car doors close brought the two of them out of their thoughts and turned their attention to the window. They could see through the curtains the people getting out, and Von took in a deep breath as her eyes landed on the little boy that looked to be around ten years old. He was the spitting image of her and though he carried the same virus that his mother did, Amir looked to be very well taken care of.

Chey watched as the man that had gotten out of the driver's seat walked around to the passenger side. Along with Amir, there were two other children, a girl and a boy. Von told her that Nivea had been married with children, so Chey assumed they belonged to her.

Slowly, the passenger door opened and out stepped a woman who had to be Nivea. She was gorgeous! Her hair was long and thick and complemented her brown skin. She was tall, but her husband was taller and made her look short. They watched as he put his hand to her face and held her with a smile on his face. Pulling her closely, he entangled his fingers into her hair and rubbed from the bottom of her neck and slowly moved his hand up. The simple gesture held so much love and affection in it that

Nivea's shoulders began to slump. He was saying something to her that was only meant for her to hear because his mouth was so close to her ear. Nodding her head up and down, she replaced the sadness on her face with a smile and kissed her husband's lips.

"Lord, send me one of them," Chey said in her head. At least she thought it was in her head until she heard Von say, "Me too, Jesus!" and fell out laughing.

They watched as only Nivea and her husband headed towards Chey's front door, and they both took a deep breath when the doorbell rang. The kids stayed in the yard playing and laughing. Nivea thought it was best that they got to talk first before the kids were brought in. They hadn't told Amir where they were going in fear of him being let down by his mother. Leaving Von in the living room, she walked over to the door and pulled it open.

"Hi guys, I'm Chey. Come on in," she told them. She watched the way they moved and as soon as they crossed over into her home, she closed the door. Turning around, she bumped right into the back of Nivea.

"Oh my God, I'm so sorry," she apologized. Nivea looked so nervous and she noticed her hands were shaking like a leaf.

"Oh no, that was my fault. I'm sorry. I guess my nerves are in overdrive," she smiled weakly. Chey reached out to Nivea and held her hands.

"God has done a mighty work in her. I don't know who she used to be although I have read her files and talked to her about her past. But the woman that she is now is nothing like that anymore. She's taken accountability for everything and even repented of all of her sins. You helped her in that area," Chey let a shocked Nivea know.

"What do you mean?"

"Because you forgave her, she was able to forgive herself. I know that things will never be like they used to be, but you can start fresh today." Letting out a deep breath, Nivea smiled and gave Chey a quick hug. It may have been her first time meeting Chey, but Nivea could feel the power of God all over her. She knew that God had put the right person in Von's life to make sure that she would be alright.

"Babe, you ready?" her husband asked her.

"Oh yeah, I'm so rude. This is my husband Terrance," Nivea introduced them. She didn't realize that he was just standing there while she was having her moment.

"It's nice to meet you in person. Did your mother really name you after some food?" Terrance asked amused.

"Terrence! You make me so sick asking that. Rude self," Nivea fussed.

"It's okay," Chey laughed, "I get that every time someone asks me my name and I tell them."

Walking ahead of them, she led them towards the living room. Von was still in the same place looking out of the window, and they all knew that she was focused on her son. The last time she had seen him was the day that she was released from the hospital after his birth, and taken back to the jail. The only things she had of him were the pictures of him growing up. She closed her eyes and almost went back into a depression with the realization of how her stupid mistakes were affecting her child. But just as she was about to turn around and say she couldn't do this, Nivea spoke to her.

"Hey Vonnie," she said in a near whisper. Von's head snapped around as the tears fell from her eyes, hearing her friend call her by her childhood nickname. Her body was almost to the floor, but Nivea got to her before she could hit it. It was as if everything had come rushing back to her and her emotions were all over the place.

"I'm sooooooo sorry Niv! God knowssssss, I'm so sorry! You didn't deserve what I did to you and I don't know how to make it up to you," Von sobbed. The scene was a very deep one for Chey. The pain and hurt that radiated from the both of them as they rocked back and forth holding on to one another, was just what they needed to get past their past.

"Shhhh, Vonnie. It's okay. We are alright. You have to pull it together for Amir, sweetie," Nivea comforted her. It was amazing to see how this woman who had been betrayed in the worst way, could comfort and console the person that was behind that betrayal. That was truly the power of God and He was the only one who could make that happen. With everything that Chey knew about the situation, she didn't know if she could be as strong as Nivea was in that moment. True enough they had gone years without seeing each other, but still. Chey just knew that Nivea was certainly cut from a different cloth.

After a few more minutes of them talking quietly between the two of them, with both Terrance and Chey watching, they got up off of the floor. Tears were still falling but they looked to be somewhat relieved. Like the tears cleansed them in some way.

"Do you think he will want to see me?" Von asked referring to her son Amir.

"He didn't know we were coming here today," Nivea said. That shocked Von and Chey. They just knew that he had been told who they were coming to visit. To know that he was in the dark about it made Von tense up again, only for Nivea to hold her hand tighter.

"He knows who you are. We have never held that information from him. Mir is such a smart boy and he has such an old soul," she laughed lightly. "All he ever wants to know about is when you would come to see him. We didn't know the answer to that. The last letter I wrote you, we never got a response and I didn't hear anything until we got the call you were out. The last thing I wanted to do was tell him that we were coming to see you and you not be really ready or change your mind at the last minute. I know he's not my child, but I will protect him until I take my last breath," she finished, and Von understood where she was coming from.

The last thing she wanted to do was get his hopes up and then to be let down if Von wasn't ready. And for a while she wasn't sure if she was ready or not. She had changed her mind so many times before, until this last time Chey wouldn't let her. She kept it one-hundred with Von and basically told her to get out of her feelings, and for once, do what was best for her and her son.

"I'm ready," Von said as Nivea turned to Terrance. Nothing needed to be said as he walked out of the room and went to the door.

The three of the women sat in silence, waiting for the moment of truth. There was no going back and the day Von had been waiting for had finally arrived. She was about to have her son back in her arms for the first time in years. It seemed like an eternity before they heard the door close and footsteps coming in their direction. Von couldn't help but to hold her breath as she waited.

First came a pretty teen with long dark hair and a face that resembled Nivea's, followed by a boy that had to have been around Amir's age. He was the perfect blend of his mother and father. Von had never even seen pictures of their daughter, Messiah, or son, TJ. It was sad that she was doing so much to hurt Nivea that she wasn't even there when she gave birth to her daughter. That thought alone made her almost lose it again until she heard the shaky voice of her baby boy.

"Mommy?"

Von's head snapped around while her hands came up to cover her mouth. The tears that began to fall were a mixture of fear, remorse, and sadness. But none of those emotions that her tears carried over powered the biggest emotion that she felt: love. The love she felt looking into the face of her baby boy was something that she had never felt with her own mother. That was part of the reason that she was in the shape she was in right now. At that very moment, she knew that if Amir would allow her, she would give him more love than he could ever imagine his mother giving him.

"My baby," Von said just barely audible as she stretched her arms wide and Amir ran right into them. He held on like he was scared that if he let her go she would disappear again, but that was one thing that he would never have to worry about ever again. His mommy was there to stay and she was going to be the best mother a child could ask for.

"God I bless your name. Thank you, Jesus," she said as she rocked her son and held on to her new beginning.

16

Chey sat back at her desk going through her files of the probationers that she was going to need arrest warrants for. Some thought that since she was young and had a pretty face that they could get over on her. She wasn't new to this, she was true to this, and someone had to wake up mighty early to get over on her.

Once she had gotten that all squared away, she reached for her cell phone that had been dinging with notification after notification from her Facebook page. Someone had uploaded the video of her singing a few days ago and it had gone viral. People were commenting on her timeline all day about how she blessed them, and even a few were led back to Christ. If anything, that was the best thing that she had heard all day.

Scrolling through her inbox messages, she noticed one that had come from Qyree. It was sent some hours after the show had ended the other day. How did he find her online? She was sure he didn't know how to spell her name and she doubted he remembered her last name. Getting over the fact that he indeed had found her, she focused on what he had written. He simply said that he needed to see her. She didn't know what on earth it could have been about and she wrecked her brain thinking of what it was. At first she thought it was about the video but at the time of his message, it hadn't been uploaded online yet. She thought back to the timeframe and he should have been with his 'companions' but there he was messaging her. Chey was glad that she hadn't responded that day because if he was needing to spend time with her that late at night, it could only mean he wanted one thing. But then, something was telling her that it wasn't about that.

Chey quickly responded, asking him if he was alright and where did he want to meet. Before she had time to take that last part back, she had already hit 'send'.

Sighing a sigh of relief when she noticed he wasn't online and hadn't been since sending her the message, she figured that she would have time to get her nerves together before she saw him again. Wait, why did she need to get her nerves together. She had been around Qyree plenty of times before but this time she was nervous and didn't know why.

Maybe it was because of how he looked at her when she saw him, or how he studied her while she was ministering at the showcase. Whatever it was it was different, and she didn't know what to expect. She had just closed her messenger and put her phone down when the door to her office opened up.

"Hey superstar," Von said smiling and carrying in takeout trays. It was at that very moment when the smell from the containers hit her nose and her stomach sounded like an African safari.

"Girl, bye. I am not a superstar," Chey said reaching out for what she already knew was her lunch.

"Well, that's not what this video with over 2 million views and a hundred thousand comments are saying," she told her, shocking Chey. She hadn't even bothered to look at the numbers the video was doing. She was just glad that people were responding to God the way they were. She may have been the one singing but He was the one that got the glory.

"Anyway, what's going on?" she asked as she dug into her food. She paused for a second to pray because she had been so hungry that she began chewing knowing good and well that she didn't bless her food.

"I just got my keys!" Von squealed and Chey did her best to join in the excitement with a mouth full of food, without choking.

It was a moment that they had been waiting for and it was finally here. All of the praying and fasting they had been doing on behalf of Von, had opened God's floodgates of heaven and her blessings were overflowing. Von had landed a good internship at the Lowndes County Health Department with the help of Chey that had the potential to become a permanent job once she graduated. With that job and a good reference from the school and from Chey, she was able to land her apartment and it would be ready by the time she would be released from the halfway house. But the biggest blessing of them all was that she now had her son back in her life and was given a second chance to be the best mother she could be.

The day that Nivea brought Von's son to meet his mother was the day that Chey saw a woman make that final declaration that there was no turning back to her old ways. Just the look in her eyes as they held on to one another said it all.

Amir was the sweetest little boy and Chey could tell that Nivea and her husband Terrance were raising him to be a well-rounded young man. He had all A's on each report card, he was into sports, and even was a part of their youth dance ministry at the church they attended. Amir even helped other kids who faced the same struggles he did with his illness, and he never let it get him down. He said it made him just like his mommy and he wasn't mad at her for it.

Von wanted so bad to have him with her full time, but she didn't want to snatch him from his environment and the life that he was used to. She wasn't able to take care of him like she wanted to just yet, and it would be selfish of her to expect him to move with her right away. She let him know that it wasn't because she didn't want him, but because she wanted the best for him, and staying with Nivea and Terrance a little while longer was best. They had come up with a visiting schedule and would see how that worked for them, and once Von was fully self-sufficient then they would go from there.

After the excitement died down a little, they ate silently while in their own thoughts. Von's thoughts were of her new beginning and Chey's mind was consumed with thoughts of Qyree.

"What you over there thinking and smiling about?" Von asked. Chey hadn't even realized she was smiling until she was called out on it.

"Nothing," she simply stated as she took a sip of her Arnold Palmer.

Von sat back and crossed her arms giving Chey a knowing look. Something was on her mind and she had a feeling of what it may have been.

"You called Qyree yet?"

Chey's eyes got as wide as saucers as she unwillingly gave herself away. She tried to keep a straight face but the muscles in her jaws betrayed her.

"Mm hmm. I knew you were feeling him. So when do I need to get my dress ready to be your maid of honor?" Von asked biting into her food.

"I thought you didn't like him when you met him," Chey reminded her. It was true that when she first saw him there was something that she felt was off, but now she knew that it was just him not trusting anyone.

"I didn't, but that was me all in my flesh. I thought he was going to try and holler at me and I just wasn't in the mood. I can admit I was wrong. Even after seeing that little episode he had with the three blind mice, something said give him a chance."

Chey couldn't help the laughter that erupted from her when Von called those girls that. She was the queen of petty but it was so funny at the same time.

"How in the world do we go from me talking to him to us walking down the aisle? Where they do that at? And you know you wrong for talking about those girls like that."

"Guh, bye! It ain't like you getting any younger and I know those eggs 'bout to dry up if you don't use at least one of them," by now, Von was laughing so hard she almost choked.

"That'll teach you," Chey laughed. There was no way that marriage was on the horizon, and especially with Qyree.

He just wasn't the marrying type, she felt like. She had been taught for as long as she could remember that if a man wanted to be a husband, he had to act like one long before he made it to the altar, and vice versa. A woman couldn't be a wife once she said 'I do'; she had to be that before the ring. If they behaved in that manner then when God finally presented the one to the other, it wouldn't be so hard for them to handle their responsibilities. The only way an athlete could become an MVP is if he exemplified and embodied the qualities that were needed to hold that title. You can't be what you haven't practiced to be and expect to reap the benefits of something great. Marriage was hard work and you had to clock in long before the ring was placed on a finger.

"I'm for real though," Von said, clearing her throat and removing the tears from her eyes. "A blind man can see the chemistry between the two of you.

She was right. There was definitely chemistry between them and that was evident since the first time she met him in college. But the moment she saw how he handled women with little to no respect, she couldn't put herself in that kind of situation. Chey didn't think he was a bad person, she just felt he may have been misguided in some way. She knew he was capable of changing with the help of the Lord, but only if he wanted to change. Until then, it was just nice seeing him.

Chey was raised in the church and her parents always told her the importance of her body being a temple unto God, and that she should wait until marriage to have sex. Even when all of the girls around her were venturing out and experimenting with different things, Chey would always remember what her mother told her.

"Baby, no man will respect your body if you don't even respect it. Giving your heaven away to every Tremaine, Denarius, and Hakeem you meet, will only show them they can defile you because you allow it," her mother schooled her. She was 13 at the time and to this day, she remained a virgin. It was during that time that she decided to stay that way until marriage because she knew the value of not only her body, but her self-worth. Any man that stepped to her had to come correct or not come at all, and Qyree definitely wasn't that one.

"I can't lie, Qyree is fine, but I need more than a tall glass of water to quench my fleshly thirst. If he can't fill me up spiritually, then he can't fill me up with anything else," Chey said raising her eyebrow to emphasize what she meant by the latter part.

"Man, where were you when I needed to hear this talk. The only talk I got from my mother was how to make sure I didn't slip and fall as I twirled my body around a stripper pole at 13," she shook her head sadly. Although she chuckled when she said it, there wasn't anything funny about what she had just said. Her mother Candace was an Evangelist by day and a madam by night, pimping out her young daughter in a strip club. Von had a hard life but she was steady making a change.

Once again, they were consumed in their own thoughts, just as Chey's phone dinged with a notification. Completely forgetting she had messaged Qyree over an hour ago, her heart felt like it had dropped to her feet as she looked down at a message from him. She was so scared to open it because she knew that he could see if she read it or not, and if he had said something that she wasn't prepared to answer, there was no way that she could ignore him.

"Tell Ree I said heyyyyy bro!" Von laughed.

"How you know it's him?" Chey quizzed.

"'Cause I just messaged him and told him you were thinking about him," she said with a straight face.

"You. Did. Not!" Chey squealed and Von fell out.

"Nah, I'm just messin'. But I did tell him you would be free around this time when I saw him at school a little while ago," she said standing to throw her stuff in the trash to leave. Her lunch break was almost over and she had one more class after she left the clinic for the day.

Totally missing what Von had just said about seeing him at the college, she hurriedly opened the messenger app and read it silently before saying, "You told him where I worked? Ohhh I'm going to get you!" Chey did her best to act like she was mad, but deep down she was kind of excited.

Shrugging her shoulders, Von stuck out her tongue as she snatched the door open. Chey was looking for something to throw and Von wasn't waiting around for it. Turning to run out of the door, she was stopped immediately by a smiling Qyree.

17

Qyree checked his messenger for what felt like the millionth time, but the only message he was looking for was from Chey. His message had gone unanswered for days, but it was still unread as well. That gave him a little room to relax. Had she read it and not responded, then he would have panicked. There had to be some way that he could get in touch with her and as soon as the thought popped up, so did another one.

He remembered the day he ran into Chey with her friend she told him they were there registering her for classes. They didn't say what classes, so he didn't even know where to begin scoping the campus, but it was worth a try.

Hopping in his car, he made his way over to the school. It was almost ten in the morning so the campus life was in full affect. Stepping out, he looked around and decided to head in the direction that he first saw them. He may not have done everything right in life, but he hoped that something he had done good would be enough to give him just a little favor at that moment. After rounding the corner and heading into one of the buildings, it looked like his favor was in full effect as he saw her.

"Hey Shawty, hold up," he yelled behind Von.

She almost didn't turn around because she didn't think whoever was behind her was yelling for her attention. No one knew her like that and that was the way that she liked it. Right then, she didn't need many people in her life while she was trying to get it back in order. Against her better judgement she turned around anyway to find Qyree behind her.

"Hey. Qyree, right?" she greeted. Of course she remembered his name, but she had to put up a front. There was no way she was about to let him know that her girl was talking about him like that.

"Yea. I'm sorry, I don't remember your name."

"It's Von. So what are you doing here?" she wanted to know. From what Chey had told her, he lived in Atlanta and there was nothing coming up around town pertaining to his company, so that could only mean one thing. He was on the search for Chey. Von knew it was only a matter of time before he returned, she just didn't know it would be this soon.

"I was wondering if you could give me Chey's number. When we met up last, I didn't get a chance to ask because of everything that was going on."

"Mm hmmm, you were entertaining The Three Stooges," she smirked.

Qyree couldn't help but to laugh at her; she was definitely a character, but he liked her.

"Yea, well Larry, Moe, and Curly got dropped off and got the boot at the same time," he said staring off into space. Von was shocked. To hear that he only dropped them off contradicted the interaction he shared with them at the event, as well as what Chey had filled her in on. She watched him for a few moments before speaking to him.

"Chey is at work but she will be going to lunch around noon. I'm heading over there in a few minutes to take her some lunch. I'm sure she'll be glad to see you," Von smiled. No matter how Chey tried her best to front, she could tell her friend liked Qyree, but she was very protective of her heart and her body. If he didn't or couldn't come correct, that was his loss.

"Don't tell her I'm coming, I want it to be a surprise," he pleaded with his eyes.

"You just better not make me regret helping you. I don't know much about you except what I saw, and that wasn't favorable. But since I believe in everyone getting a chance at least once, I will help you out. Don't get it twisted though, Chey may be *real* saved but I'm fresh off the yard," she said with a straight face. Qyree knew she was serious and for some reason, he wanted no parts of that.

"Nah man, you good. I 'preciate it," he said jogging back towards his car once she gave him the address. He needed to handle a few things before he got to her, to make sure their encounter would be one she would remember in a positive way.

Before he had the chance to get his seatbelt on, his phone was ringing. Not bothering to see who it was before he answered, he cringed as soon as he heard the voice.

"Qy! Where are you?" Natalia yelled through the phone.

"That's none of your concern," he told her with one of the nastiest tones he had ever given anyone.

"Oh really? We supposed to be kicking it but I can't ask my man where he is?"

Removing the phone from his ear, Qyree looked at it with a confused face. There was no way that she had just said that to him after finding out what she had been up to. She must have eaten something in Cancun that made her lose her mind.

"Man, go 'head on! You come up to the house where my mother lives and expose the affair that you are having with my father, and now we were in a relationship. Shawty, you wild," Qyree fumed. Even though he had left as soon as he saw Natalia, he later learned from his mother what she was doing there. To say he was shocked would have been an understatement.

"*Had* an affair," she said like that made it any better. "If you had answered your phone you would know that already."

"Listen, I'm cool on you. It never was an 'us' and even if there was a possibility, you blew that one," he said sucking his teeth and pulling up to a flower shop. He had planned on bringing Chey some flowers, something that he had never done for a woman, and invite her out to dinner.

"Come on baby, don't be like this. I didn't even know he was your daddy," Natalia lied. She knew that man was his daddy because she was sleeping with him first, but now wasn't the time for her to divulge that piece of information.

"Aight. It don't even matter though. I got somewhere to be," he told her while the lady behind the counter totaled up his purchase. Qyree had no idea what her favorite flower was, but he decided to get something other than the normal roses.

"Who is she?" Natalia asked. It sounded like her words were getting choked up in her throat and he knew darn well she wasn't about to cry. Off jump, she knew what it was when they met and she was cool with it. No need to get brand new and let some feelings develop that were definitely not mutual between the two of them.

Not even bothering to answer her question, he hung up the phone in her face. She was talking crazy and he had to get himself together. He didn't know why he was feeling the way he was, and the feeling had Qyree so far out of his comfort zone. But he figured with everything else going wrong in his life, this could possibly be the one thing that could possibly go right.

He wasn't far from Chey's office which was a good thing. Looking at the time, he figured that he had wasted enough time driving around, and headed to the building of the address he was given. Checking his messages real quick, he saw that he missed a notification. His cheeks began to hurt as he saw it was from Chey. The fact that she was concerned if he was okay or not did something to him. She had asked him where he wanted to meet her and as he got out, he replied he was already at her job and 'bout to walk in. Von gave him the directions to her office and just as he was about to knock, the door came flying open to a pleased Von and a shocked Chey.

18

Six Months Later

"Hello?" Chey answered her work phone. She had just a few more things to take care of before she could enjoy her four-day weekend with her bae, and she couldn't wait. This would be the weekend that she would be introduced to Qyree's parents as his girlfriend.

To say that Chey was surprised by the relationship would be an understatement. The Qyree that she had met in college and even the one she reunited with a few months ago, was a totally different Qyree than he was now. His past may have been one that should have turned her away from him, but it was something deeper there that she couldn't deny. During the week, it was hard to see one another, but they had been making it work and she was happy. When she wasn't on the phone with Qyree, she was spending time with Von, who just so happened to be on the other line.

"Hey sis!" Von said. It had been such a blessing to be around Von and watch the changes that she went through for her son. Amir was now coming to see her twice a month, holidays, and would be staying with her once the summer started. The love that little boy had for his mother was unreal, and Chey couldn't wait for her time to become a mother.

Many would have thought it would be a tough transition for the two of them, being that Von was missing out on so much of his life. But God had a way of lining everything up where it worked out for everyone involved. He had placed Amir with two people who were after His own heart, when He put him with Nivea and Terrance. Now that Von was no longer in the halfway house and in her own, she could finally be the mother that God called her to be. Chey was so proud of her and they had really become like sisters. Even the three of them would hang out a bit when Nivea would come to drop Amir off.

"What you doing?" Von asked.

"Just finishing up in the office before I call it a day. I was just given a new file so I was trying to go over it real quick before I leave," Chey told her.

"Girl, if you don't go home and get ready to spend time with your boo you betta! I know he can't wait to get you all to himself," Von laughed.

"Unt uh, you know it's not like that with us... yet."

"Ooohhhh, you gonna be fassss this weekend, huh? You better do it then sis!" Von cackled.

"No, nut! You know we not going down that road. I need a ring and a husband before that jumps off."

Von sucked her teeth and laughed because she still found it unbelievable that Chey could still be holding out.

She felt like one of them had to get some so the other could live through the other, and they knew it couldn't be her. There was no way that she could get involved with a man, tell him her status, and he would stick around. So she would just focus on her baby boy and live through Chey and Qyree's relationship.

"I know, girl, I'm just messing with you."

"Hold on sis, let me get this other line. It's like they know I'm trying to get out of here by noon and they finding every reason to stop me," Chey said.

"Well go ahead. I got to get back to work anyway. Don't forget to call me when you see your surprise," Von said excitedly before hanging up. She knew what she was doing by telling her about a surprise, but not telling her what it was.

Before she could even begin to wonder what the surprise could be, the line beeped again. Taking a deep breath she was prepared to tell anyone that needed her to stay later than noon 'NO'.

"Hello?"

"Heyyyy giiirrrllll!"

"Natalia?" She hadn't heard from Natalia since she called and said that she wouldn't be able to make her performance, and that was almost six months ago. Every time Chey would try and reach out to her, she was too busy with her man. Chey still didn't know his name.

"Don't act like you don't know your best friend's voice," Natalia scoffed. She knew it had been a while since she had been around, but all of that was about to change.

"So what's going on?" Chey asked ignoring the 'best friend' comment. They had fallen off so bad it wasn't even funny. Von had been more of a best friend lately than Natalia.

"I'm coming down that way this weekend so we should catch up," she said smacking her gum all loud.

"Well, we are going to miss each other because I'm coming to the city," Chey said looking over the new file. Her breath seemed to get caught in her throat as she looked at the name and mugshot of the person.

"Did you hear me?" Natalia asked annoyed.

"Hum... wha...what? No, my bad, I was looking over this file before it was time to go. What did you say?"

"I said what you coming to the A for?"

"Oh, bae is bringing me to hang out. We haven't had much time lately so since I have these few days off we're going on a little getaway," Chey informed her, getting excited all over again. She decided to close the file and reopen it when she got back to work. The last thing she needed was anything that took her away from her man. She just prayed that the information in that file was all a coincidence and not at all what she was thinking.

"Bae? Since when this Miss Stiff Booty get a man? I was beginning to think that you were waiting for Jesus Himself to come down and marry you," Natalia laughed like she had just told the funniest joke in the world, but she was the only one that found it humorous.

"And if I was waiting for Jesus to come marry me it would happen before anyone decided to marry you," Chey shot back, putting an end to the laughter. Chey may have been saved and loved the Lord, but she had a little petty still stored away for the days that people decided to get cute.

Before either of the two ladies could say anything else, there was a quick knock on her office door followed by Qyree's handsome smiling face. Immediately, all of the attitude Chey had been feeling seconds before thanks to Natalia, was now gone.

"Hey beautiful. You ready?" he asked coming further into the room. His scent reached her nose even before he got close to her and she couldn't help but to close her eyes and enjoy it.

"Is that—" Natalia started but was cut off.

• "Bae is here so I'm about to head out," Chey said not giving her time to respond. Quickly, she put in the code that she needed for all of her calls to go to voicemail and to let the caller know she was out of the office.

"Oh, so you finally decided to tell your other man about me?" Qyree laughed walking over to Chey.

"Mm hmm. I figured it was time that he knew he was replaced with something better," she smiled, as he wrapped his arms around her waist.

"Say word. I got the top spot now?" Qyree smiled. Chey loved the way the corner of his mouth would turn up when he was happy. It was something small but it was so big at the same time.

"Well not the top spot. You know that belongs to God."

Turning his lip up and squinting his eyes as if he was thinking, he finally said, "I can play that position. But that's the only one I'm gonna play second to," he said seriously.

"You're such a big baby."

"You love this big baby though," Qyree said stopping suddenly, noticing what had just come out of his mouth. The both of them held their breaths because neither had said those three powerful words to one another yet. It was something they both felt but didn't know if the other felt the same way. Qyree was quietly waiting on her response and Chey was quietly wondering how he would take her response.

"I do love my big baby," she almost whispered but he heard her. Looking into her eyes, he knew that she meant it and he prayed she could feel it from him as well.

"And your big baby loves you more," Qyree said honestly, as he pulled her closer to give her a kiss.

Chey had sealed the deal on the direction that he was willing to take their relationship and she didn't even know it. She was the first woman besides his mother and late grandmother, Norma that he had ever said those words to and meant it from the bottom of his heart. Even when he was playing the field, he had never uttered those words just to get what he wanted from a woman. He had seen how those words affected his mother when his father said them, but then his actions would show something totally different. Although he never saw himself getting married and he really didn't respect those women, he would never get her hopes up about having anything with him other than something physical.

Speaking of physical, this was the very first time that the two of them had been this intimate. Of course they held hands or hugged, he had even given her a few pecks on the cheek, but their lips had never collided until now. The power that he felt through that kiss was like nothing he had never experienced, and he wasn't sure what this woman was doing to him. Everything that he thought he knew was nothing like he was living.

The type of women that he used to run around with weren't even worthy of his lips touching theirs because he knew what they did with those lips. Nothing he did with them was intimate or meaningful like he was doing with Chey, and it kind of made him a virgin in a sense. Not the physical sense because that was gone a long time ago, but everything he was doing was new with her. She was bringing a side out of him that he never knew could exist.

He didn't know if he was just tired of the life he was living, or if God was opening his eyes and heart. Could have been both. Either way, he was ready. From the first day she had crossed his path again, she was constantly on his mind. And when she got on that stage, she broke something in him that she wasn't even aware of. When he left Fatima and her girls at their house and the other girl at the hotel without hopping in the bed with either of them, he knew why. Chey had somehow woven her way into his heart without his permission, but he found himself accepting her in.

"Come on, let's get out of here. I have a surprise for you," he said, unwillingly breaking their kiss.

"Is this the same surprise that Von told me about?"

"Man, sis can't keep her mouth closed for nothing. I bet I don't tell her anything else," he pouted.

"Aww, don't be mad, she didn't tell me," Chey laughed.

"She lucky my nephew gonna be there this weekend or I'd go cuss her out," he smirked.

"And she will cuss you right on back out too. With y'all potty mouths."

"Wait a minute, I'm getting better with that I thought. You know the Lord ain't through with me yet," he said trying to look offended.

Chey couldn't help but to laugh at the face he was making. She had to give him credit in that area though. Since he had been spending time with her, going to church, and even spending time with her father, Qyree was really trying his best to be a better man. Not for her, but for himself first. Before he could be the man that she or any woman needed, he had to learn how to be a man first.

She knew that inviting him to church with her in the beginning didn't mean a thing. That was something that women didn't seem to understand. Just because they wanted a deeper relationship with God didn't mean the man they were with or trying to get with wanted the same thing. Inviting him to church didn't mean a thing if it wasn't what he wanted. So many times that theory ended up backfiring on the woman because the man ended up leading her away from God. They would use the fact that she loved him so much or his opinion mattered to her so much that he could sway her thoughts from the church. A man should want that relationship with Christ for himself, and not for any other reason. That went for the woman too.

Qyree was tired of the logic he was given from Jaxon about God, and was finally returning back to what his mother had tried her best to instill in him. He wasn't a stranger to God, but he hadn't been in his face for some time and if he wanted to lead a better life than what he had been, it was time. All of the cars, clothes, money, and women were getting old, so when he popped up at church one day unbeknownst to Chey, he had been coming ever since. He made sure that if he had gotten busy and couldn't make it down the night before, then he would get up real early on Sunday and make that trip in time to make it to Sunday School.

"You're right, baby. He's still working on the both of us 'cause I'm struggling to keep these thoughts cast down," she said trying to pull away from his embrace but he held her tighter.

"Say word? What thoughts?" He knew what she was feeling and he was too, but they weren't ready. He was going to do this relationship right for the first time in his life. He just liked to see her squirm a little.

"Unt uh boy, let's go. You are not about to make me speak those things that are not as though they were." Her imagination was running wild and the last thing she needed was to speak those impure thoughts into existence.

"They gone be one day though," he said sharing a laugh with her. The look on her face was one of trying to figure out if he was serious or not. Pecking her one last time on the lips, he grabbed her hand while she grabbed her purse. He wasn't about to answer the question lingering in her eyes with words, he was just going to have to show her with his actions, he thought, as they headed to spend what neither of them knew would be one of the most memorable weekends together ever.

19

As soon as they had put her bags in Qyree's car, they grabbed something quick to eat and got on the road. She didn't have to worry about her car considering the fact that she had let Von use it while she was out of town. Von was still trying to get established and didn't have a car, so on the days where she needed to do a lot of running around, Chey would let her borrow hers. Any way Chey could help Von and make sure she didn't go back to her old ways, she would.

Canton Jones was playing through the speakers while Qyree drove and Chey read a book on her Kindle. In the past, you couldn't get him to listen to gospel music, but here lately that's all he played. Praise and worship music had graced his speakers a few times, but not as much as the gospel rap did. He related a little more with those lyrics, not to mention they were still upbeat enough for him to groove to.

"What you reading?" Qyree asked, turning the music down some. Whatever it was had her attention and her finger constantly swiping the screen.

"This book called _Damaged Goods_ by Jenica Johnson," she replied, never taking her eyes away from the words she was focused on. It almost sounded like she was in a hurry to tell him so that she could focus back in.

"You mean the one where that girl Shy was catching the beat down by that dude Amond, or something like that?" he asked. This time he saw her look at him out of his peripheral with a shocked look.

"Ahmod, and yea, that's the one. What you know about this book?" He could hear the smile in her voice.

"What, I can't like to read?" he asked faking like he was offended.

"You can read, but I didn't know you would read this type of book."

"You mean a Christian book?"

"Yea. I took you for a street or urban reader," she said. Her assumptions would have been dead on a while ago, but now those books didn't appeal to him anymore.

"I've always liked to read and you're right, I was into those type of books. But now it seems like they are all the same. And since kicking it with you, some of my interests have changed, that being one of them," he explained.

"I agree. I still read a few urban books but not as many as I used to. These Christian books have really stepped up their game over the last year or so. They are so relatable to everyday life and still give you a good message, too."

"Yeah. That's true," Qyree said as Chey went back to reading.

He couldn't wait until they got to Atlanta. He had so much planned for them to do, including dinner with his mother. Zaria was so excited when she found out that the two of them had reunited and were now in a relationship. She made sure to tell him every chance she got when he would come by the house, how he'd better not mess this up. She had always liked Chey and to know that her son had a woman like that in her life made everything she put up with worthwhile.

Qyree didn't go by his parents' house as much as before, but he talked to his mother every day. The moment Natalia popped up at their house that day, it was a done deal for him. He hadn't been anywhere near his father or the office since then and he only talked to Jaxon by phone, where it concerned the company. Even then, Qyree wasn't in the mood to talk considering the fact that the position he was working towards was snatched away from him by someone he didn't even know.

Shaking his head, he still couldn't believe how his father had played him but he should have seen it coming long ago. Qyree had lost count of the many times his father went back on his word if the situation wouldn't be beneficial to him. He was sick to his stomach the day that he found out his father had been sleeping with Natalia. The moment his mother told him everything, it became clear that both Natalia and his father had played him. Qyree had taken her to a couple of company events in the past, nothing major, and had never introduced the two. In fact when he thought about it, every time he wanted to introduce them he would look up and Natalia would be missing. For them to have hooked up meant that Jaxon had seen them and went after her or he was already messing around with her. Jaxon knew his son and knew how Qyree treated women. Jaxon just had no idea how that one decision would change his world forever.

Chey was glad that they would be beating the Atlanta rush hour traffic by the time they got into town. She absolutely hated being at a standstill for sometimes hours, waiting to get to her destination. That's one of the reasons she chose to stay in a smaller town. The city life just wasn't appealing to her and she didn't think it ever would be. If the relationship between her and Qyree was taken to another level and marriage was involved, she didn't know how he would take the fact that she didn't want to live there for the rest of her life. Would that be a deal breaker for them? Deciding to put those thoughts to the back of her mind, she focused on the scenery.

"So what is this surprise you have for me?" she remembered, and turned to him smiling. She was so anxious and didn't know if she could wait any longer to find out what it was.

"You'll see in just a few minutes," he said, not giving her the answer that she was looking for. Chey was the worst when it came to surprises. She couldn't wait to get them and she couldn't wait to give them. If it was someone's birthday, she would give them their gift all early. She felt like because they expected a gift on the day, that it wouldn't be a surprise at all, so she would give them out days before. She was weird like that.

"Can I get a hint?" she asked.

"The hint is you're going to love it," he laughed.

"That is not a hint." Qyree laughed at the pout on her face as he grabbed her hand and gently kissed the back of it.

"Just hold on lil' mama we almost there. I promise it will be worth it."

"It better be," Chey smiled.

"Have I ever let you down before?" he asked seriously. He knew that this relationship was new for the both of them but when he made the choice to pursue Chey, he already knew he had to come correct. She wasn't like the women he was used to so he did his best not to mess up what they were building. Chey challenged him to be better whereas his jump offs only challenged him not to strangle them for getting out of line.

"No baby, you haven't let me down," she smiled and went back to her reading.

20

About twenty minutes later, they were pulling up to a construction site in Smyrna. The building looked to be about 75 percent done and the way the men were moving around, it wouldn't be long before they were complete. It was three stories high and stretched across the lot. If the outside was any indication of how the inside looked then Chey knew it was going to be beautiful.

"What's this?" Chey asked getting out of the car and walking closer to get a better look. She wanted to see what was on the inside, but knew that it wasn't safe to enter just yet.

"My surprise for you," he said walking over to her. The look on her face told him that she was clearly confused.

Taking her hands in his, he just held on to them as he looked around the building then back at her. He wasn't sure how she would react to what he was about to tell her, but it was now or never.

"I had always wanted to start a gospel label under Hype Lyfe but my old man was against it. Both me and my mama tried to get him to see the bigger picture but he was too against it. Felt like it was a waste of time and money. Anyway, when he pulled that stunt on me after the showcase I knew it was time for me to make moves on my own," he said.

"You mean when he gave the position away that you earned?"

Nodding his head to her question, he continued.

"When that cat got on stage rapping about God and then you followed behind him blowing us all away, I felt like that was a sign to step out on faith."

"So you were finally able to convince your dad?"

"Nah. This is all me. I gave him my resignation letter a while back and took the money that I had saved up and started the process to open my own gospel label," he said shocking her.

"Oh my God, baby! I'm so proud of you!" Qyree had told her what he wanted to do for a while, but she never thought he would go that far and actually do it. She had been praying for God to lead him and it looked like her prayer had been answered.

"Thanks, Chey. It was a big step and I'm still not too sure how it will all work out, but I'm going to give it a try. I mean, as long as you stand by my side," he said to her with a questioning look.

"Of course I have your back. What are you going to name it?" she asked.

"I'm not sure yet. I was hoping we could come up with something together. And who knows, maybe you can record your first platinum album and put us on the map," he laughed lightly, but she didn't join in with him. Immediately at the sound of stepping into the studio again, Chey felt like she was going to be sick. She was just good with supporting Qyree on this new journey, but the past that she still wasn't over was slowly creeping its way into her present.

Qyree watched her demeanor change yet again at the mention of her being in the studio. This wasn't the first time he brought it up and her mood changed suddenly. She would get this far away look on her face and her breathing would become rapid like she had just run a mile. Each and every time he asked her what was wrong, she brushed it off and he knew that if he gave her the opportunity to blow it off again, she would. Before they went any further in their relationship, he needed to know what demon she was fighting and how he could help her to get over whatever she had gone through. Qyree may have been new and starting over in his walk with Christ, but he knew the power of prayer, thanks to Chey. Saying a quick and silent one, he moved closer to her and wrapped his arms around her and just stood there. Nothing had been said between the two of them for close to ten minutes, before she finally opened her mouth.

"My mother had one of the most amazing voices that I had ever heard," she began. "As far back as I could remember, when she would tuck me in at night she would sing this little song she made up."

Qyree said nothing as he observed the side of her face. She still had the same faraway look in her eyes, but she was now smiling as she thought about her mother.

"I love you a bushel and a peck, a bushel and a peck and a hug around the neck. A hug around the neck. And a barrel and a heap, a barrel and a heap and you make my life complete…" she sang and trailed off. The tears that were falling down her face wouldn't allow her to continue, and Qyree was unsure of what to do so he held her tighter.

"I was six years old when it happened. All my mother talked about was becoming a singer. She wanted nothing more than to sing to the glory of God, but my father was against it. He felt like if she got discovered then she would leave him and find someone better. He didn't think that she wanted to do it to make a better life for us all. So she snuck behind his back and started going to the studio. It wasn't often because she couldn't afford booking time on the regular because she didn't want my father to know.

This particular day, she decided to take me with her. I had been begging to go for so long and she had finally given in. I wouldn't dare let my father know because I knew he would be mad and not let me go again. My mother told him that we were going to the store for something for dinner, but we ended up at the makeshift studio that her friend had set up in her basement. Ms. Janice's brother lived with her and they had dreams of making it into the music business, and they knew the talent that my mother was gifted with would set it off," Chey paused.

"Have you ever shared this with anyone, Cheynese?" Qyree asked her. She knew he was serious because he never called her by her full name. All she could do was shake her head no.

"I'm listening, bae. I got you."

Taking a deep breath, she continued with the most difficult part of her past.

"I still don't know how my daddy found out where we were, but he did. When my mother heard him yelling from the front of the house, she made me hide. There was a table in the room that had all of the equipment set on it, and it was covered by a big black table cloth that touched the floor. Mommy didn't want me to go under it just in case it fell, so she made me go behind it and be quiet.

I'll never forget the look of fear in her eyes as she told me, for what I didn't know would be the last time, how much she loved me. As soon as the words left her lips, the first shot rang out. Sheer terror covered both of our faces as she told me to be as quiet as I could. She turned to run out of the room when the second shot became closer than the first. God, I was so scared I wet my pants and prayed that he didn't smell the pee. If he did, he would know where I was."

By now, she was shaking and trembling inside of Qyree's arms so bad he had to take her and sit her in the car. Kneeling down beside her, he did his best to comfort her. He should have known it was something horrible by the way she acted, and he was now kicking himself for prying. Had he known it was going to be this bad, he would have left it alone.

"Chey, baby, I'm so sorry you had to go through this and I only made it worse asking you to talk about it. I'm so, so sorry baby," he apologized as she shook her head.

"No. I needed to get this out. The haunting has been so bad for almost twenty years and I can't keep letting the enemy attack me in this area any longer."

Taking a deep breath and wiping her eyes, she finished.

"Don't get me wrong, my daddy was a good man. He took care of home and we never had to worry about a thing. That was until he lost his job down at the chalk mine that he was working at. It seemed like everything went downhill after that. My parents constantly argued about Mommy going out and getting work, but he was dead set against it. He was the head of the household and if she was to go out and work, that would look like he wasn't handling business. So when she kept bringing up the singing, he thought she was trying to leave him. I would never forget the night I lay in my bed and heard him tell her in a tone neither of us had heard before, that if she tried to leave him, he would kill her. That day in the studio, he kept that promise," she said looking Qyree in his eyes, and his heart felt like it was being ripped out of his chest. No longer was she crying and her breathing had become normal again.

"Mommy ran out to try and stop him or to calm him down, when they began yelling back and forth. She was telling him how she just wanted a better life for us and how she didn't mind helping. That's what God put her in his life for, to be his help mate. He wasn't trying to hear anything that she was saying and then all of a sudden it got quiet. I started to move from my hiding place, when I heard my mama scream before there was another shot. Scared still, one last shot went off and the sound of death in that house was louder than any sound I have ever heard."

Qyree was at a loss for words as he tried his best to comfort and console Chey. Looking at her on the outside, you would think that she had it altogether, but she was really in a constant battle on the inside. He couldn't imagine having to face what she had faced at such a young age. To see his mother and father fighting over a woman was as bad as it had gotten for him, but Chey had to experience the loss of not one, but both of her parents.

They sat outside the building a few more minutes before deciding to go and get settled in for the night. He had a date night planned for them but after the bomb she just dropped, he knew that all she would probably want to do was check into their hotel room and chill. That was fine by him, because as long as he was in her presence, that was all that mattered to him. He could do nothing for the rest of his life but as long as he was doing nothing with her, he would be satisfied.

Shaking his head, he kissed her head and shut her door so that he could walk around to his side of the car and get in.

"I'm sorry Qy, for dropping that all on you like that," she said bringing him out of his thoughts. All his life, he had been taught to care only about his feelings and in this moment, he realized that everything wasn't just about him. There were so many people who were hurting, especially the women he used, but there were even more people who failed to pay attention to the needs of others. That wasn't what God put them here for.

It was then that Qyree made the conscience decision to repent for all of his sins. He couldn't go another day being as selfish as he had been and with God on his side, he knew that he could be a better man than he had been. People never realized how their testimonies, as bad as some were, could be that one thing that stood between someone else and Christ. He hated that Chey had to endure so much pain, but there was purpose in it. A powerful purpose at that.

Pulling out of the lot, Chey welcomed Qyree's hand inside of hers and she felt like such a burden had been lifted by getting that horrible memory out. While her healing may have just taken place, Qyree couldn't help but to feel like something was on the way. A raging storm was brewing and it was headed right for him.

21

Since Chey's revelation the day before, Qyree decided to wake up early and have breakfast delivered to her in bed. He could only imagine how tough it was for her, so he wanted to do whatever he could to bring that smile he loved so much back to her face.

They had a suite with two bedrooms so after the three chick flicks she made him watch, she ended up falling asleep on him. After making sure everything was secure, he eased out of her room and decided that he too would call it a night. He wasn't even pressed about sleeping in the same bed as her and he could tell that she was shocked at how he responded to her when she let him know. Yeah, his old ways may have preceded him, but he was all about trying something different. It was never too late to change and for him, a future with Chey was his motivation.

Picking up the phone, he was glad that he had been paying attention to what she liked to eat. Qyree was glad that she wasn't shy around him when it came to eating like most of the women in his past. She said she would rather get full than be around him with her stomach sounding like a mating call in the wilderness. That was something else he loved about her. Chey had a sense of humor out of this world and kept him laughing.

Thirty minutes after he placed their order, room service was knocking on the door. He knew she was still asleep by the sounds of the trees being sawed down in her room. Chuckling to himself, he opened the door to a bad lil' mama on the other side. Her body was on point and her face wasn't half bad either. She was definitely someone he would have tried to make a pass on under normal circumstances, but it amazed him how he felt nothing. For the first time in his life, Qyree really felt like he had found the one. If Chey could make him pass up making a new notch in his player's belt and giving up that playboy life, she had to be a keeper.

"You ordered breakfast, handsome?" the girl whose nametag read Rena, asked.

"Sure did," Qyree said keeping it short and pulling out a twenty for a tip.

Holding her hand out to stop him from handing over the money, she said, "No need for that, but I wouldn't mind your number instead."

It's funny how now that he was trying to change his life around in a different way, women throwing themselves at him was no longer appealing to him. Since being back in Chey's life, seeing how she carried herself, and him getting closer to God, his outlook on life was different. Did he get close to slipping a few times? Absolutely, but he was able to catch himself before he messed up the blessing that had come into his life.

Smiling politely, he shook his head and replied, "No thank you, sweetheart, my lady won't appreciate that much. I appreciate you bringing us our breakfast though. You be blessed," he said closing the door.

Chey had been awakened when she heard knocking at the door and as hard as she tried to come out of her slumber to get it, she just couldn't move fast enough. She had hoped Qyree didn't hear her snoring because she was sure if he did, it would be a turnoff for him. She had left her nasal strips at home by accident, so she knew it went down while she was asleep.

Opening up to him the way she did the night before had drained her, but it was much needed and for the first time in years, the dream that haunted her did not replay itself as she slept.

By the time she made it out of the room Qyree was already at the door and she could hear that he was speaking to a woman. When she declined his money and asked for his number, the first thing she felt like doing was making her presence known, but just as fast as that thought came it left. If Qyree was serious about them as he had declared, then he would handle this situation accordingly. A relationship had to be based on trust and if she didn't trust him, there would be no reason for them to move forward. The last thing she wanted was for him to feel like she didn't believe he could change and continue to hold his past over his head. If God didn't remind Paul that he was a murderer, who was she to remind him of the man he no longer was.

Hearing his response to the young woman made her heart swell, and she silently thanked God. She didn't thank Him for Qyree claiming her as his woman, she thanked God for the turnaround in his life. She prayed that even if they didn't last forever, Qyree would stay on the right path. He was so much more than what he thought he was and she hoped he could see it as well.

Chey hadn't even noticed he was looking into her smiling face until he was right up on her. She had been so deep in thought about him.

"What you smiling at? I know ya boy fly early in the morning. I woke up like this," he said standing back and striking a pose.

Chey couldn't help but to laugh, but suddenly stopped when she realized she hadn't brushed her teeth yet and instantly covered her mouth.

"Yea, you might want to throw something around in that mouth real fast before you do all that laughing. Almost burned off my beard; you know how long it took me to get it like this?" he laughed.

She punched him in his chest with a closed fist, as he faked pain.

"That was not funny! My breath is not that bad," she pouted as he walked closer to her and put his arms around her waist.

"If smelling your hot breath for the rest of my life guarantees me that I have you for the rest of my life, then that's what it is," he said sincerely placing a soft kiss on her lips. "Now hurry up so we can eat and get out for the day before we have to go to dinner at my parents' house."

Chey saw how his mood changed that fast and instead of calling him out on it, she nodded her head and walked over to the food. Looking down in awe, she smiled. He had been paying so much attention to her and what she liked, and the breakfast before her said that. Chey loved her eggs scrambled soft with cheese and steak strips, a side of hash browns topped with mushrooms, and a bowl of strawberries and cantaloupe. She had to have a cup of Tazo Passion tea each morning or her day started off on the wrong foot. For him to think of her in such a way meant so much to her, and she could see this relationship was

heading in the right direction. So why was her gut telling

her something was about to try and knock them off course?

22

Jaxon sat in his office looking over the paperwork that sat on his desk. He was so overwhelmed with work that he hadn't had a day off in what felt like years. As soon as Qyree turned in his resignation letter, things went downhill. Jaxon didn't think about what his son's reaction would be once he told him he was giving his job to someone else. He felt like since Qyree was the best man fit for the job, he would continue to work in the same capacity as he had been doing all of these years. In fact, he had been the reason that they had all of the hottest acts that they had now, but that wasn't enough to give him the position he was working for. That position belonged to someone else and come hell or high water, he was going to sit in it soon.

Now, it didn't bother him at first that Qyree quit, but the moment he found out he was starting his own label, Jaxon flipped. There was no way that he was going to allow his son to outshine him. That was the main reason that he wouldn't let him get that spot. Had he been given that title, all eyes would be on his son instead of Jaxon and he wasn't having that.

"Mr. Reeves, your wife is on line one," he heard his assistant speak through the phone. Not bothering to reply, he simply picked up the receiver and pressed the button to bring Zaria on the line.

His marriage was rocky before, but it was even worse now. He could only imagine what she wanted being that she hadn't said one word to him since she came back from the doctor a week ago. She had one of the nastiest attitudes known to man and that was another reason why he had been staying downtown in his condo with Natalia. She, too, was getting on his nerves with all of her nagging and whining, but she always knew how to please him when he was stressed. That's all that mattered to him anyway.

"Yea Zaria, what's up?" he asked with an obvious attitude.

"Don't forget Qy and his friend are coming over for dinner. Do you think you will have time to jump out of the trashcan you been laying up in long enough to find your way home?" she shot back, matching his attitude. He could tell that she had been drinking by the way she was slurring her words.

"I'll be there," he said and hung up in her ear. If Zaria was already drinking, then he knew it would only be a matter of time before something jumped off this evening, and he wasn't looking forward to it. The only reason he was going was because he wanted to let Qyree know that he wouldn't make it in this industry without him, and either he gets back on board or risk getting blackballed. Jaxon was such a force to be reckoned with that he knew his reach would be far. There would be no one that would want to associate themselves with his son if he had anything to do with it.

He hurriedly got his things together and decided that he would come back to the office after this so called dinner. Not wanting to miss the chance of speaking with Qyree, he made his way to his condo as fast as he could, to change, hoping Natalia was out and about. That way he could slip in and be gone before she got there to nag about where he was going. That's one thing he missed about his wife, she never questioned him. He didn't know if it was because she didn't care or because she didn't want to hear the truth, but she never bothered.

"Where you going?" Natalia asked, walking into his bedroom and throwing herself on the bed. Had he not gotten caught up by his secretary when he was trying to leave, he would have been out of the house five minutes ago. Shannon had been feeling neglected since he had been busy with work, and she wasn't about to let another day go by before she got her a piece of him. Who was he to continue denying her?

"Going to the house to have dinner," he said as he buckled his belt and grabbed his wallet, sticking into his back pocket.

"Oh, so no invite? When you gonna stop hiding me like this? It's not like your little wife or even Qyree don't know about us," she said getting up in his face. Natalia was starting to feel so used but had no one to blame but herself. She had been using men for their money all of her life, and always got what she wanted, and now that things weren't going in her favor, she had an issue. First, Qyree showed out on her and here his daddy was trying to still hide their situation. Yea, she was wrong for messing with a father and son, but they were wrong for playing with her emotions like they did. Both making her think that she was something special only to drop her like a bad habit.

She watched him grab his keys and head out the door without saying a word to her. That was it, the straw that broke the camel's back. Since he didn't want to see things her way, she would take matters into her own hands. Picking up her purse and own set of keys, she locked up and headed to her car.

Let the games begin.

23

Qyree and Chey had one of the best days either of them have had in a long time. Just being able to kick back and have fun with one another was something that they would rarely get to do for a long period of time. It wasn't like they never had fun, whenever they were together for a quick date or he was just passing through, it was ever a dull moment. They had just wanted the fun to last longer than it normally did and now their wish had been granted.

After breakfast, they headed downtown to Underground Atlanta, made a stop at the Georgia Aquarium, had lunch at T.I.'s restaurant, Scales 925, and got a few hours of shopping in. Chey had even gotten Qyree to go and get a pedicure with her. He was so against it at first, but after some convincing, he finally obliged. Not long after they sat down, she understood why he was against it, he was ticklish. Chey had never laughed so hard before a day in her life, but Qyree was not amused. The look on his face was a mixture of humor and agony and that made it worse for Chey. He had tried giving her a death stare, but the little Asian woman wasn't letting up on his feet so all his look did was make her laugh harder.

Leaving out of the mall, it was close to four in the afternoon and they knew the trip from where they were in Atlanta to Sandy Springs where his parents lived, was about to be a hectic one. As soon as they got on the highway, it was gridlocked. Looking over at Qyree, Chey noticed that his upbeat mood had suddenly changed and it had nothing to do with all of those cars. He was stressing about being around his father again after everything that had transpired. Finding out the affair his father was having with a woman that Qyree had messed with in the past, as well as him not telling Jaxon about his new company, was enough to stress anyone out. Chey hated seeing him like that and since he was there for her in her time of need, she felt like she needed to do something to ease his troubled mind, even if it was only for a few minutes.

Pulling out her phone, she pressed a few buttons on the stereo and making sure her Bluetooth was turned on, she paired the two devices and got ready to turn up. When the music came through the speakers, she turned the volume up and got into her zone.

"They know Zoo Gang with me, turn off all these cameras please. Step up if you gone bang at me just know I got that thang on me," Chey rapped along with Fetty Wap's "Decline". She already knew Qyree was looking at her in shock, so she kept going.

Qyree watched Chey mess with his radio so he knew she was about to play some music, he just had no idea it was about to be Fetty. He couldn't help but to laugh at her while she acted like she was straight out of the hood. She was going in word for word with a hard look on her face like she was a straight gangster. Chey was pointing her fingers in the air like she was talking to someone who was about to catch those hands and that's when he lost control of the laugh that he was trying his best to keep in.

"Man, Chey, you wildin'," he laughed at her. "What you know bout Fetty?"

"Boy, bye! Just cause I'm in the church doesn't mean I have to listen to gospel all the time," she told him. It was a big misconception when people thought that once they got saved they could no longer listen to secular music. Chey was one that felt like if the music or songs took you down the wrong path, then you may need to leave it alone. Some people weren't strong enough to handle anything other than gospel or inspirational music, and that was fine too.

They laughed, talked, and even discussed the direction that Qyree wanted to go with his company. Before they realized it, they were pulling up to the gate of his parents' house. Chey saw him begin to get tense all over again, so she reached over and grabbed his hand. She tugged on it just a little bit so he would know that she wanted him to look at her. When he did, she saw the uncertainty on his handsome face.

"God got you, bae. Whatever happens tonight, know that it was in His will and I'm here with you, okay?"

Squeezing her hand back and leaning over the center console, he gave her a kiss on her cheek. Hearing her say that she would be there with him through it, eased his troubled mind. He took a deep breath, let it out, and drove up the winding driveway to the front of the house. Chey thought it was beautiful on the outside so she could only imagine what the inside looked like.

Before either of them could get out of the car, the front door opened and his mother stepped out with a smile on her face. To Chey, she looked just as gorgeous as she last remembered, and the smile spread across her face enhanced her beauty. But Qyree knew different. Zaria was lit and gone off the bottle. He could tell by the way she held her mouth and her eyes were glazed over. From that point forward, he knew things were about to go left and quick, once his dad got there. It was going to take every prayer from both he and Chey along with all of the angels, to prevent what was about to jump off. Why his mother wanted him to bring Chey if she was going to be drinking was beyond him. He was hoping that what she said in the car a few minutes ago would still ring true in about an hour.

"Hey my baby," Zaria squealed running out to them. Qyree couldn't lie and say that he wasn't happy to see his mother because he was. He just hated to see her in this condition. He moved towards her with open arms just as she ran past him like he was invisible and embraced Chey.

"Say word. You just gonna do me like that?" Qyree asked trying his best to look offended. In reality, he was beyond happy that his mother was accepting of Chey the way she was.

"Oh hush, child. I can see you when I want to but I haven't seen my daughter-in-law in years," she said as Chey smiled.

"How you just claiming people as your daughter-in-law. How you know Chey even feeling me like that?" he asked and winked his eye in her direction. Chey couldn't deny the butterflies she was feeling no matter how hard she tried to.

"I knew she was going to be your wife the first time I met her. I was just waiting for you to get your stuff in order. Anyway, enough of that, let's go inside," Zaria said leading the way.

Just like Chey had thought, the inside of the house was even better than the outside. The marble floors were so clean, Chey could see her face in them and she probably could have eaten on them too. The art that adorned the walls had an Afrocentric feel to them and each one that Chey passed gave her a deeper look into her roots. At least that's what she felt like. Qyree held her hand as they followed behind Zaria and made their way into the sitting room. She just knew they were about to walk into one of those all white rooms that rich people had in their house for show that the guest weren't even allowed to breathe hard in. So she was pleasantly surprised by the room that was decorated in earthy tones of browns and gold.

"So you finally got my boy to settle down, huh?" Zaria said as she sat down.

"I wouldn't say all of that. I mean, a woman can't make a man do something he doesn't want to do unless it's in his heart, right?" Chey asked.

"This is why I love her. So smart. I'm glad you waited to find the right one before you brought her to meet me," she said, shocking Chey.

"You mean you've never brought a girlfriend home to meet your parents?" she looked to Qyree and asked. He simply shook his head no like it wasn't a big deal, but Chey thought differently. Qyree was nearing 30 years old and to find out that he never introduced anyone to his parents until now was big.

"I never felt anyone to be worthy of that. All I wanted to do was see what they were working with, not get married. That's all I knew," he said honestly. Before anyone could comment on what he had just said, they heard the front door open and immediately knew who it was.

Chey watched how both Qyree and his mother's demeanors changed at the same time, once the man she assumed was his father walked into the room. Zaria looked like she wanted to cut his head off and feed it to alligators, and Qyree's handsome face was full of disgust. The air in the room began to feel like it was slowly leaving the room, as she waited on someone to speak first. Since they didn't, she did.

"Hi, I'm Chey," she said reaching her hand out to shake Jaxon's. The lustful look he gave her as his eyes roamed over her body made her so uncomfortable, and Qyree was quick to jump on it.

"Aye man! Don't you think one is enough?" he asked referring to Jaxon messing with one of his former flings. He didn't care what they did in the past; he was not about to let his father get any ideas about Chey.

"My apologies," Jaxon said, but deep down Chey felt like he didn't mean it.

"So what am I here for, Zaria? I need to get back to the office and finish up work that my son should have been doing had he not been in his feelings about a little job title," Jaxon said.

Chey watched as the two men eyed one another like they were about to square off at any moment, and she wasn't sure if it would end well. Silently, the two women watched the interaction between father and son, waiting to see who would make the next move.

"Well, if my father would have given me what I earned then maybe he wouldn't have to be working late and he could be on another remote island booed up with another one of his son's side joints. You know, since you like sloppy seconds and all."

"You mad or nah?" Jaxon asked being petty.

"Nah," Qyree said as he grabbed Chey's hand in his and ushered her into the dining room. He needed a few seconds away from his father before he forgot that he was the man that raised him.

Shaking her head while giving Jaxon a menacing glare, Zaria turned around to follow Qyree and Chey into the other room. She knew that if she didn't hurry up and let them know why they were all there, she may not have the chance to. The last thing she wanted was for Jaxon and Qyree to get into it, and she have to tell them separately.

Zaria figured they all wanted to know why Chey needed to be there and under normal circumstances, she wouldn't let outsiders into their affairs, but she didn't look at Chey as an outsider. Sooner or later she would be her son's wife, and she was going to be the only one who would be able to help her son through this difficult time. She couldn't count on his father to do it because he was the reason she was making this announcement in the first place.

Chey looked around at the spread on the table and her mouth began to water. Neither of them had eaten since lunch and her stomach was reminding her at that very moment. Fried chicken, baked fish, candied yams, macaroni and cheese, mustard greens, potato salad, BBQ ribs, fried corn, the list went on. It was like Thanksgiving in the middle of the year and Chey wondered who else was coming to dinner. This couldn't possibly be just for them but if it was she had no problem taking a few to-go plates back down the road. Her and Von could be set for the next week with as much food that was laid out.

"Dang Ma, who else coming?" Qyree asked thinking the same thing.

"Nobody, but feel free to take as much home with you as you would like."

"Bae, where's the bathroom so I can wash my hands?" Chey asked just as the doorbell rang. Thinking nothing of who it could be, Qyree busied himself with showing Chey where the bathroom was, while his mother went to the door. Jaxon just stood there like he was so impatient and ready to go. If he didn't feel like this was really important, he would have been gone already, but he still needed to talk to his back stabbing son about the new company he was starting. If that conversation didn't go as he had planned, then Qyree would leave him no choice but to blackball him. It was Jaxon's way or no way.

"Jaxon, your little trollup is here again. She got one more time to pop up at my house unannounced," Zaria said walking away from the door and leaving it wide open. "But since you are here you might as well come hear what I have to say too. Considering this is probably some mess you started."

"Qy, what are you doing here?" Natalia asked as soon as Qyree walked back into the room.

"I could be asking you the same thing but since I don't care and you are no longer my business, I'ma stay in my lane," Qyree said unfazed by her presence. He hadn't fooled with Natalia in a hot minute since she popped up on their door the last time, so he was good on her.

"Why are you here?" Jaxon screamed on her. This was the last thing he needed right now. Her showing up right then the way she had, was about to make things so much worse. The looks that both Zaria and Qyree gave her when she walked in were priceless. He had wanted to avoid this for as long as he could, but here she was making a scene yet again.

"Because I'm tired of you thinking this is okay. You need to come clean about—" Natalia started only to be cut off.

"Nat? What are you doing here?" Chey asked walking back around the corner. All eyes went to Chey while her eyes went to Natalia's overgrown belly.

24

Natalia knew as she followed Jaxon to the home that he shared so many years with his wife, that things were about to get crazy. She just had no idea how bad they were going to get. It was like God was steady telling her to turn around, but she ignored Him and listened to the devil that was riding shotgun. She wished God had shown her what was about to happen instead of just telling her to turn away, but what lesson would she learn in that? Either she was gonna listen or not and quite frankly, she doubted she would have turned away even if He did reveal it to her.

She knew that she was wrong for messing with father and son, but she was out to get what she wanted by any means necessary. The night she accompanied Qyree to an industry party she almost peed on herself when she saw Jaxon there and every time Qyree wanted to introduce the two of them she made sure to not be around. Either she had to use the bathroom or she needed something to drink. The last thing she needed was for Jaxon to blow up her spot. As the night went on she thought that she was in the clear. That was until she really did have to go to the bathroom and bumped right into Jaxon.

Thinking it would be hard to keep them in the dark about one another, proved to not be an issue at all. Jaxon let her know that night that he wasn't worried about her messing with his son as long as he got what he wanted. With Qyree only coming around when he needed that one thing, she was able to balance the two. That's why Qyree felt that she was so easy to get along with and didn't expect much from him, and she didn't. Well not at first. Jaxon was doing everything she needed so there wasn't a need for her to be pressed about what his son was doing. Only when Jaxon started being distant after she told him she was pregnant, did she lean towards Qyree more, just for him to play her too. Natalia didn't know if it was her hormones making her feel strongly for Qyree or if she had really caught feelings. That all changed though the last time she saw him. He had some nerve coming over to her house with another broad in the car with him, and had her out there looking stupid and fighting. He may not have known she was pregnant at the time, but it was still not a good look. Her nosy neighbors still gave her the side eye going on seven months later. Since her ego was bruised, she was going to return the favor.

Her whole plan flew out the window the moment she saw Chey walk into the room, and the look of shock on everyone's faces spoke volumes.

"Chey, what are you doing here?" she asked.

"Unlike you, she was invited," Zaria said, with each syllable she spoke laced with venom. Natalia couldn't stand her and didn't care nothing about the fact that she was the mistress and not Zaria. If anything, she was the one entitled to having an attitude because she was carrying the next heir to their royal empire.

Rolling her eyes, Natalia refocused her attention back to Chey, waiting on an answer, only to be hit with another smart remark from Zaria.

"Sit down you little troll. You might as well hear what I have to say considering I'm sure it has something to do with you, too."

"Well if she stays then Chey and I are leaving," Qyree said walking over to where her best friend stood. They may not have been as close as they had been, but she still considered them to be besties. However, from the look of pure disgust displayed on Chey's face, she knew that friendship was a wrap.

"So this the new lil' boo you tried to hide," Natalia said.

"And with good reason, too," Chey shot back.

"Girl, tell me you not still mad about Calvin," she scoffed.

Calvin was Chey's first love back in the ninth grade. They met in the church that both she and Natalia grew up in and were getting pretty serious by their junior year. When it came time to go to the Junior/Senior prom, Calvin thought that would be the night that he turned Chey into a woman, but she was not there for it. Calvin may have played the role of the innocent church boy who was still a virgin, but he hadn't been a virgin since the fifth grade. The only reason Natalia knew that little bit of tea was because she was the one who assisted him in that area.

No one knew about what happened between the two of them and no one ever said a thing up until prom night. Throughout the years, Calvin wanted to take things to the next level with Chey, even though he was getting his needs met elsewhere the whole time. It was just something about Chey that he yearned for. Maybe it was the fact that she was pure in every sense of the word, and that was appealing to him. To know that no other boy had had the privilege to experience the heaven she possessed was what continued to draw him to her. But as soon as Chey told him what wasn't about to happen, he flipped out on her and aired out all of he and Natalia's dirty laundry, causing the two girls to fall out.

Being that they went to the same church and were practically sisters, eventually they got back on track before graduation. Chey was big on forgiving and moving forward; she just made it a point to never bring her man around Natalia again, especially if they were serious. But life had been so jam packed with school and working, Chey hadn't pursued anything with anyone until now. Seeing Natalia brought back memories that she thought were gone but from the look on her face, the past was rearing its ugly head again.

25

Zaria walked over to the bar and poured herself another drink. She had lost count of how many she had thrown back, but she was still the only one in the room that looked unbothered. This wasn't how she had planned to spill the beans, but so be it.

"So I called you all over today… well, all of you except the trash that the garbage man forgot to take out to the landfill," Zaria said with a roll of her eyes. Natalia returned the nasty look with one of her own. To be sitting in the house of the woman whose husband and son she was messing around with and have an attitude, just further let both Chey and Qyree know that they were better off without her in their lives.

"I know you are all wondering why I stayed with Jaxon for so many years knowing all along he was no good.

Well I'll tell you. He wasn't always a good for nothing whoremonger. In the beginning, he was so humble and loving. He treated me like I was somebody and not just a quick romp in the bed. It was me who was there to help him get started with his dream and once it became a reality and the money along with the women came into play, here I was being thrown to the side.

Night after night, I cried and I prayed that he would change, but what did he do? He poured his venom into our son. See, I knew that I couldn't teach my baby how to be a man. That was something only his father could do, and by the time I figured out the type of man he was molding my baby into, it was too late. Qy, baby," she said getting his attention.

Turning to look at his mother, he remained quiet. He didn't know what she was about to say but he was beginning to feel like everything he had eaten in the past year was about to come back up at any moment.

"The last thing I wanted you to ever see or feel was that I was a weak woman. I know it may have seemed that way and with everything you were learning, it didn't make me look any better."

"Oh, cut the crap Zaria! You not about to stand here and feed my son lies just to make yourself look good," Jaxon jumped in. He was fuming mad and it wasn't just about this little charade his wife was putting on. Everything around him was starting to take its toll but he wasn't about to take all of the blame.

"Isn't that what you've been doing his whole life? Lying to him to make yourself look good. What kind of man raised his son to be a hoe?" Zaria yelled throwing her glass full of liquor in his direction.

Before Jaxon had a chance to respond, the doorbell rang again.

"You sure you don't have anything you want to tell Qyree before you open that door?" Zaria challenged. All eyes were on him as he looked around clueless. That feeling that both Chey and Qyree had been feeling was now intensified. Whoever was on the other side of the door was already causing more problems and no one had even seen their face.

"Chey, baby, can you get the door for me, please?" Zaria asked. Chey was shocked as to why she wanted her to do it, but she obliged anyway. She could hear Jaxon and Qyree's mother going at it as she pulled the heavy door open.

"Hi," Chey greeted as normal as she could. She wasn't sure who the woman and man was that were at the door, so she hoped they would either leave or not be too thrown off by all of the noise.

"Humph. Jaxon must have him another one," the woman said pushing past Chey and walking into the house with the man hot on her heels. The two of them looked like they were on a mission and it was one that Chey wished God would step in and abort.

"Well look who we have here. If it isn't the help and her bastard child," Zaria said looking around her husband at the two people who had just walked in.

Chey noticed the look on Qyree's face and he looked like he was about to snap at any moment. Natalia tried to be funny as she walked over to try and touch his arm so that he would calm down, but Chey wasn't having that.

"Heffa, I wish you would touch him," she said walking over to where he was standing. Natalia knew by the tone of Chey's voice she wasn't playing no games, so she backed down without a fight.

"What are you doing here, Toni?" Jaxon asked when he noticed them in the room.

"Zaria called us over," the woman named Toni clarified.

"Yes I did," Zaria told him while getting excited. "Since you claim to have always been upfront with Qyree, have you told him that the person you were putting in that A&R position was your illegitimate child? The one who you have been grooming since birth to take over your company one day?"

If looks could kill, Jaxon would have been two stepping into hell by now, by way of Qyree's glare.

"This is unbelievable. I don't even know what to say to you right now. Come on Chey, let's go," Qyree said pulling her by the hand.

"Qy, wait! What are we going to do about the baby?" Natalia blurted out causing them to be frozen in place. If Qyree thought for one second he was going to ride off into the sunset with his new boo, then he had another thing coming. She knew good and well there was no way that Qyree could be her baby's father because the dates didn't line up, but he didn't have to know that.

"You know good and well that's not my baby," he frowned.

"So I slept with myself?" she asked, crossing her arms over her stomach like it was a prop. Since Chey thought she was so holy and no harm could come to her, the news of this baby would give her a rude awakening. She expected Chey to storm out of the house by her little so called revelation, but the joke was on her because the woman before her looked as cool as a cucumber.

Not bothering to reply to her comment 'cause he already knew what she was doing, he began to walk away again. He couldn't believe that his father's motto "It's all about the heaven between her thighs" would cause this much hell in his life. He now knew he had messed up but nothing could prepare him for the next thing that his mother said out of her mouth.

"Natalia, you and the help here," Zaria started as she tilted her head towards Toni, "may want to go get tested before you have that baby. I'd hate for him to be born into this world like his step mommy."

"What are you talking about?" she asked with an uninterested look on her face.

"I'm so glad you asked," she said throwing a pill bottle on the table near Jaxon.

"Truvada? What is this?" he asked, picking the bottle up to read the label.

Chey knew exactly what it was because Von took the same medicine.

"It's used to treat HIV/AIDS," she said as Zaria took the whole bottle of Hennessey to the head.

To Be Continued.......

Be sure to check out new music by Waycross, Ga's own Mike Murk on Reverbnation!!

Facebook: Mike Murk

Made in the USA
Columbia, SC
22 December 2018